JARED

MELISSA BELLE

Autumn Ink Press

Cover Art: J. Hunter Designs
Proofreading: Dawn Yacovetta

ALSO BY MELISSA BELLE

Boston Boys
BOSTON BILLIONAIRE
BOSTON LOVE
BOSTON ESCAPE
BOSTON ROOMIE
BOSTON BAD BOY
BOSTON PLAYER

Wild Men
COLTON
DYLAN
AYDEN
JENSON
BRAYDEN
CAMERON
DECLAN

Wild Men Texas
WHISKEY GIRL
WARRIOR GIRL
WILD GIRL

Storm Brothers
HUNTER
MAX
JARED

LIAM

Bonus Wild Men Stories

WILD MAN (Colton and Sky prequel novella)

WILD VALENTINE (Ayden and Bella short story)

Sign up for Melissa's Newsletter to get a free story and to receive alerts and updates on upcoming book releases.

ABOUT

A twist of fate makes them roommates. Will they finally act on their feelings...or miss their chance forever? A friends-to-lovers, forced proximity hockey romance.

Jared Storm and I grew up friends.

No, not the kind of friends like in the movies where it sometimes turns romantic.

Jared was a star in our town, and I didn't want to shine just because of his light.

Besides, I had my own secrets to keep.

He moved away to become a hockey star, and I stayed in New Orleans.

I thought I'd live there forever.

Just like I thought I'd never sleep with Jared Storm.

But sometimes life takes a hard left turn.

And you have to be ready for the bumps along the way.

To all the brave hearts

CHAPTER ONE

Jared

I drill the puck so hard into the net that Coach whistles an end to practice.

"It's just practice. Our first game's not till later this week," my twin brother, Max, says to me as we skate off the ice together.

"So?"

"So why the crazy focus? I thought you were all about easing into it."

"I was. Things change."

"You're in great shape, Jared," our coach calls out to me. "Love the way you've come into this year. We're going to need all you've got to get back to the mountaintop."

"Yes sir."

The Montana Wild Kings had a good season last year. We didn't repeat as champions, but we went deep into the playoffs before bowing out. Individually, though, I had a down year. I don't like excuses, so I never made any.

I was healthy physically, as healthy as I ever am during a grueling regular season with all the hits and brutal contact. But mentally, I was off my game. I struggled with insomnia and anxiety late at night. I never told anyone, including Max, but this season, I'm determined to be an all-star again.

I'm a co-captain, and I take my role seriously. After Declan Wild retired and became a part owner of the team, more attention shifted to me. I welcomed it. But a part of me struggled with the added pressure. My brother, on the other hand, had his best year yet. He also fell in love—with the girl next door from our childhood.

I've stayed clear of the relationship bug that Max and my youngest brother, Hunter, caught. Both are happily involved and engaged to be married. The other night, however, I did rescue a cat. Even a furry roommate brought on issues—I was no longer welcome in the condo I'd been renting in the city for the past five years. The owner of the building couldn't have cared less about who I was, and she immediately booted me from the place. When I protested, she begrudgingly backed down and gave me three days to find a place.

"Hey," I call out to Declan on my way to the locker room. He came to watch our first practice of the year, and he's been standing outside the rink. "Thanks for letting me know about the cabin at Wild Ranch. I'm heading there tonight. My bags are packed. What's the number again?"

"Cabin eight." He hands me a set of keys. "I just texted you the directions. It's a little out of the way, which will be good for your privacy. The other cabins are all booked for the next four weeks—besides guest bookings, Mia's invited a bunch of bloggers to town for the foundation. They'll be doing trail rides and watching join-up with one of the new horses."

"Cool." I take a look at the circles under his dark eyes. "Rough week with baby Lexi?"

He grins. "Being a dad is hands down the hardest job I've ever had. But I wouldn't trade it for anything."

A pang of longing hits me in the chest. I may not be able to hold down a relationship, but being a father is something I've thought about a lot. I miss my own dad every day, and the chance to follow in his footsteps would be a dream come true.

But I see the pain that my big brother, Liam, is going through as a single dad. I don't think I'd choose to parent a child alone. Which means, at some point, I'd need to commit to a woman. And that's the part I can't imagine. I've yet to date anyone who's been able to hold my interest for more than a week.

I wave goodbye to Declan and head for the showers.

"Hey," Arch Morrison, our starting left-winger, calls out to me as I'm grabbing a towel from my locker. "You want to grab drinks with Tex and me?"

Arch and I have the same outlook on relationships. We don't have them. We party together often, and Tex, co-captain along with Max and me, likes to join us.

"Not tonight," I tell him.

Tonight, I have something important I need to do. Someone important I need to go see. I just hope she won't punch me in the nuts at first sight. Ashley Hill and I may be old friends, but we don't have a normal relationship.

However, that's what I like about her. About us. She may just be a friend, but she can definitely get and hold my attention. She always could. I break into a grin as I head for my truck.

CHAPTER TWO

Ashley

Wild West Ash

I take a selfie of myself smiling and giving the peace sign from my window seat on the airplane before hitting save on my social media account.

I've worked in marketing for years, and social media is naturally a big part of my job description. I enjoy it, but I also like clicking off when I'm not working.

I put my phone away and pull out my worn and tattered copy of My Antonia from my bag as soon as the plane takes off.

By the time we reach cruising altitude, I'm fully engaged in the story. The West always fascinated me, even though I'd only been west of Houston once when I flew to Montana earlier this year. But then my PR and marketing company was bought out by a larger one, and I was transferred to Missoula.

I honestly didn't plan to ever leave the south. But it was either accept the transfer or I was out of work. One bonus—I'll have plenty of opportunities to be around horses and to experience the true Wild West. Mia, my boss, offered me a cabin on the ranch where she and her husband live, which is a relief because the idea of apartment-hunting sends me spiraling further into overwhelm.

Mia's husband, Declan, also happens to be the minority owner of the Montana Wild Kings ice hockey team. That's a fact I've been trying to ignore all summer as I planned my cross-country move. I happen to know a couple of the players on the Kings—and one of them, in particular, I have a long history with.

My stomach flips over just thinking about Jared Storm. Thank God he doesn't know I'm moving to Montana. I'll tell him in my own time when I'm ready. First, I need to put my feet down in my new home and get settled. Jared knocks me off kilter enough as it is.

Granted, with Declan and Mia living on the ranch, I'm going to have to contact Jared sooner rather than later. But Mia told me my cabin is off the beaten path and I don't need to see anyone if I don't want to. That sounds perfect to me, and in a couple of days, I'll give Jared a call and fill him in. He lives in the city anyway, and he's about to be fully immersed in his hockey season, so it's not like I'll be bumping into him on the daily.

The plane ride is smooth and uneventful, and when we land, I take a moment as I walk through the terminal and wait for my bags at baggage claim to stare out the windows and appreciate the mountains. They're so majestic, and I can't wait to go hiking in them.

I grab my two suitcases off the belt. Unable to find a dolly, I start dragging them behind me as I follow the exit signs. I'm going to be leasing a car while I live here, but I can't sign the papers until tomorrow, which means I don't have a way to get to the ranch from the airport. However, I declined Mia's offer to come pick me up. Mia has a new baby at home, and I don't want to take up any of her precious time. I'll take a cab; I hailed enough of those in New Orleans.

Between reading the signs and glancing back every time one

of my suitcases tips onto its side, I'm not paying attention to anything else.

"Oomph." I slam into a hard body. "I'm so sorry..." I glance up, right into the amused eyes of Jared Storm.

"Wild West Ash. Welcome to Montana."

CHAPTER THREE

I stare at him, half-torn between wanting to slap him and kiss him. So, basically, my normal resting state when it comes to Jared.

He looks back at me with his naturally flirty smile. His hands are in his pockets as he waits patiently for me to acknowledge him.

Typical Jared. He's dressed down in a gray Big Easy hoodie and worn blue jeans, and he's got a black nondescript baseball cap covering his dark, thick hair. But the way he carries himself is overwhelmingly sexy. He's tall and confident with a casual air about him that screams "I don't give a shit what anyone thinks of me."

"You never look at social media," is the first thing I can think of to say.

"I had a special reason to today."

"What does that mean? And why are you here?" I drop both suitcases to put my hands on my hips. I hate that he can send me into a near-fit for no reason other than that sexy grin he's shooting my way.

"Why do you think? I came to pick you up. Even turned

down a night out with Arch to do so. That's how important you are to me."

"Please." I roll my eyes. "You mean you'd miss out on a night of casual hookups to hang out with your old friend? I feel so special."

Jared chuckles. "You jealous?"

"Never," I say vehemently. "You know I don't want to be one of your darn hookups."

He lowers his head so we're at eye level, and I hate that I break the eye contact first.

"Of course you wouldn't."

I can't help the smile pulling at the corners of my mouth, and Jared opens his arms. "There's my girl."

I step into his embrace, and he hugs me warmly. I hold onto him like a lifeline. Because that's what Jared Storm and I have always been for each other. We just hid that fact a lot better than Hunter and Winter did. We were best friends in the worst of times, although in the best of times...we drifted. It's just who we are. Jared's there for me when I need him the most and vice versa, but when we don't, we live separate lives.

"I'm happy you're here, Ash," he says in my ear.

I fight the shivers that race down my neck. I've never allowed myself to get lost in Jared Storm's orbit. If I did, we couldn't have maintained our friendship. It's difficult enough as it is. Jared plays hard, parties hard, and dates light. If we had ever slept together, it would have destroyed the rare bond that we have.

We both knew that, and we were careful to stay on the platonic side of the line. Doesn't mean he didn't piss me off all the damn time with his cavalier "dating" style. And I use the word dating with as much sarcasm as I can muster. Jared honestly doesn't understand the world of relationships. I suppose I could teach him, but the idea of helping him find a future wife sends me into a sea of envy I'm not ready to process.

He pulls back to look at me, and his eyes flash with vulnerability. "Care to tell me why you didn't want me to know you were moving here?"

I swallow. "Care to tell me how you found out?"

"Declan mentioned it to Max. I'm sure Mia knew not to tell us, but the message never got passed to her husband." He raises his eyebrows. "Why the secrecy, Hill?"

I purse my lips, debating how to answer him. "I just...I wanted to surprise you."

He narrows his gaze. "That's a lie."

"How do you know?"

"You just pursed your lips. Tell number one for Ashley Hill."

I inhale.

He leans down to kiss my cheek. "I know all your tells, darling."

My pulse picks up, and Jared licks his bottom lip. We stare at each other for three heartbeats. Until it's too hot, too awkward, too...much.

I back up a step, and Jared stands up straight. And then, we go back to being Jared and Ashley, old childhood friends who never once, in all our years together, hooked up. Except, the thing is that recently, I've felt...like maybe I wanted to. But I couldn't do a one-night hookup with Jared, and I'm sure that's all he'd be down for. I'm doubly sure it would be a colossal mistake if it ever happened.

And that's why I didn't tell him I was moving here.

Because this *right here*—this smirking, arrogant as all hell, handsome, sexy man standing in front of me as he irritatingly grabs my suitcases and starts walking like I gave him permission to help me—this is why I didn't want him to know. Not until I was settled and calm and had my shit together. Because right now, I very much do not have my shit together. I will shortly, but at the moment, I feel uprooted and homeless.

"Jared!" I really wish I wasn't wearing heels. I can barely keep up with him as he strides purposefully through the airport.

"What?" He glances over at me as I hustle along next to him.

Somehow, the suitcases never once tip over despite him walking at twice the pace I was when I was dragging them and they were tipping all over the freaking place.

"You're doing that thing you know I hate!"

He laughs. "What thing?"

"Acting like you're the boss of me."

"I don't do that."

"You do. Actually, you act like you're the boss of the universe."

He flicks his gaze toward me but doesn't slow his pace. "Of the universe, huh? I didn't think you'd mind me taking charge."

My face heats. This conversation is taking a turn I didn't plan on.

Jared and I always give each other shit. It doesn't normally turn flirty.

We round a corner, and suddenly, we're at an elevator bank. Jared presses the button, the doors open, and he ushers me in ahead of him.

We ride the elevator in silence to the parking garage, and we only walk a few hundred feet or so before Jared stops at a large four-door truck with a cab in the back.

"Did you upgrade?" I ask him in surprise.

Jared's the kind of guy who will drive his vehicle until it dies. He was brought up with humble roots, and it's one of the things I love about him. He never forgot where he came from, despite the impressive multi-million dollar contract he has with the Wild Kings.

"I did." He opens the back door and slides in my suitcases. I notice he's got a couple of duffel bags on the floor, but before I can ask him about it, he adds, "My old truck bit the dust."

"Rusty?" I put my hand to my heart. "You and that truck went through so much together." *So much loss and so much joy, too.*

He shuts the back door and leads me around to the passenger side. "Time to make new memories," he says as he opens the door and helps me in.

I look at him more closely as he hands me my seatbelt. Something about the way he said it gets my attention. "Are you okay?"

His chocolate brown eyes flecked with green look at me like lasers. "I'm okay."

"You swear?" I say as I buckle my belt.

His lips twitch. "Swear."

I relax against the seat back as Jared shuts the door and walks around to the driver's side.

I wipe my sweaty palms on my skinny jeans and unbutton the flannel I'm wearing as an overshirt. All I've got on underneath is a fitted purple tank.

"I didn't expect Montana to be so darn hot."

"It isn't usually this warm so late in the season. But there are days like this." He glances briefly at my attire. "You must have dressed up for me, Ash."

"Fuck off," I say breezily.

He breaks into a laugh. "You know I love that color on you. It brings out the violet flecks in your eyes."

I feel myself blushing, and I try—*so hard*—to pivot away from the dangerous vibe between us. "I have hazel eyes."

"With violet flecks," he repeats.

I relent. "Fine. With violet flecks."

"They're gorgeous," he adds before starting the engine. "So. Where to?"

"Um..." I force down the butterflies threatening to take over my tummy at his casual flirting. "I figured since you found out I was moving here, you'd also have uncovered what my living situation is going to be."

"Nope. I'm not that nosy." He grins at me.

I smile back at him. "Ha. Sure you're not. Just like I don't have hazel eyes."

"With gorgeous violet flecks," he says in a low tone I'm not used to him using with me.

I feel my pulse pick up. "Anyway..." *That was smooth, Ash...*

"I'm happy to hear I can surprise you with one piece of information. Maybe I can hold onto that secret a while longer?"

Jared pays at the parking gate and pulls up to the street. "You gotta tell me some time so I know whether to go left or right."

"Fine." I show him the address on my phone.

He stares at the screen. "Wild Ranch."

"That's right."

He jerks his head in my direction. "What do you mean?"

I stick my tongue out at him. "What do you mean what do I mean? I'm staying in a cabin at Wild Ranch. Mia set it up."

"Huh." He turns left. "That's very interesting."

And now I'm on edge. "What do you mean? Why is it interesting?" I tug at his sweatshirt. "What do you know, J?"

"Nothing much. It's just..." He turns the wheel to the left again, and we merge onto the highway.

It's mid-afternoon, and I get a perfect view of the mountains as the truck picks up speed. The majestic peaks distract me—so much that I nearly miss what Jared says next.

"Wait." I shift in my seat to face him. "What did you just say?"

"I said that I'm also moving to Wild Ranch. Tonight."

CHAPTER FOUR

"Hold up." I shake my head to clear any cobwebs. "Why would you leave your condo?"

"Long story short—I was out for a late-night run in the rain, and I heard an insistent meow."

I can't help the laugh that bubbles out of me. "You took in a kitty?"

"I refer to her as a cat, but yes. She was starving and wet. And she came to me when I called."

He sounds pleased with this fact, and I smile to myself. Jared's always adored animals.

"And let me guess—your building doesn't allow pets?"

"Bingo." He puts on his signal, and we exit the highway.

Within minutes, we've left the city behind. All I see are pastures of cows, enormous pine trees, and fields of wildflowers. And the mountains, which are a beautiful and constant landmark.

"So pretty." I press my face to the glass.

"I think you're going to like it here, Ash." Jared's tone is cautious.

He *wants* me to like it here. I can hear it in his voice.

"Do you love it as much as home?" I ask him curiously.

"I love it in a different way. Home is home, and New Orleans will always be my touchstone. But the memories there are... mixed. As you know."

"Yeah." I have the same feelings about the Big Easy.

Jared thinks he knows my secrets. And he does know most of them. All except for one. The one I keep closest to my heart. The one thing from my past I can't shake.

I've never told any of my friends. Outside of Mama and law enforcement, I locked my story away and pretended it didn't happen. My mother insisted it was best. And she's probably right. I've never been a good liar, though. Hiding a piece of my past has eaten away at me, and I sometimes wonder if it's changed the way I've lived and the choices I've made.

I always knew that if I ever told anyone one day, it would be Jared. A part of me feels the need to tell someone just so I'm not holding it all inside anymore. But it will change things between us forever.

I shake my head and return to the present moment. What's important right now is my living situation, which suddenly feels complicated. Living on the same ranch as Jared isn't exactly ideal when I'm trying to get my footing. He's too distracting.

"So, your first game is this week, right?" I say as we drive along the winding country road.

He nods. "Home game. You coming?"

"I'm not sure. It's also my first week of work."

"I understand. I'll leave you tickets at the front if you decide you're up for it."

"Thanks. I always love watching you play."

He chuckles. "Now you're talking shit."

I glance over at him. "Am not."

"Are too. You lose focus on my games the minute the puck is dropped."

He's completely right. I love to go to the games, and thanks to all the time I spent listening to the Storms talk about their sport, I actually understand hockey more than the average fan.

However, I prefer to chat with whoever's next to me about whatever the hell I'm in the mood to talk about that day rather than trying to follow the puck as it flies across the ice from one stick to another.

What he doesn't know—and I hate to admit this—is that I loathe watching the women fight for Jared's attention after the games. So I try not to watch him too much when I'm there in person. I've convinced myself, that way, it hurts less to be a witness to his fan girls afterward.

"I'm your biggest fan," I say, surprised at how possessive my tone sounds.

I can tell that I've surprised him too because he whips his head over and looks at me.

"Anyways..." I kick at the floorboards. "Are we almost to the ranch?"

"Just about."

Jared puts on his signal, and I glance to the right.

Wild Ranch reads the silver sign hanging from an arched overhang. We drive up to the gate, and Jared puts down his window to punch some numbers into the box.

I glance down at my text from Mia. She'd provided the passcode, but Jared obviously knows it already.

We drive along the main paved road and I marvel at the large trees on either side. When we come out from the forested area, all I see for miles are fields. Fields of horses and cattle.

"This place is enormous," I murmur. "You must love hanging out here."

"I do. Going horseback riding and on hikes is refreshing."

"Whatever happened to your coach wanting you to keep your feet on the ground when you're not on the ice?" I tease him.

He smiles. "I got my agent to make an exception for riding."

"Did you really?" Jared doesn't do something like that unless it's really important to him. He is a rebel for sure, but he loves his job too much to break too many rules.

"At first, I thought, 'What he doesn't know won't hurt

anyone.' But then, I thought better of it, and I approached my agent with the idea. Coach said he gets that request more than he'd like being in Montana, and he always wants to say no. But he was okay to sign off on it." He points at a ranch-style home off to the right. "That's the main house where Luke, Chase, and Cooper live."

Right, the three Wild brothers. I met them through Winter when we came to Montana last year. I remember they have a fourth brother too—Brayden—but he lives on his own ranch in a neighboring town. Their parents retired and left the family business to Luke and his two brothers to run.

"Where to?" Jared asks me. "There are cabins all over the property. Do you know where yours is?"

"Um..." I glance down at Mia's text. "She says take a hard left at the fork."

Jared glances down at his own phone and furrows his brow. "Are you sure?"

"That's what it says." I recheck the text.

He puts down his phone and turns the wheel sharply. We take almost a hundred-and-twenty-degree turn onto a dirt road.

We drive along for about a mile until the view of a log cabin on a crystal-clear blue lake opens before us. The lake is small, and the cabin is the only structure in sight.

"Wow." I look over at Jared. "Do you think that's my cabin?"

"It's the only one on this road."

I bounce up and down on my seat. This is *amazing*. I'm going to live on a real western ranch in a log cabin. And I can ride horses every day and actually get paid to take photos of them for social media. I can't believe my luck.

"I'm never this lucky," I say out loud as Jared parks the truck next to the cabin and we hop out.

But it looks like I am today.

Because the cabin is perfect. Private but safe. Far from people but close enough that I can call on the Wilds if I need anything. And I trust them because I trust Mia. And Jared loves them.

Jared grabs my suitcases and carries them to the front door of the cabin for me.

"Thank you," I tell him sincerely. I reach into my purse. "I have the key in here somewhere..."

I've got my head down while I fish through my mess of a handbag. So when I hear a click, I don't recognize the sound at first.

I pull out my key and look up to see the front door to the cabin is already swung wide open.

"What the heck..." I look up at Jared.

A key dangles from his thumb and index finger.

I hold up the key in my hand.

They're both unusual keys with a long silver arm and a deep cut at the base.

And they freaking match.

"What..." I say weakly.

"Funny thing..." Jared leans his shoulder against the wall of the cabin—*my* cabin. "Declan told me I would be living in cabin eight."

I have no idea where he's going with this until he tilts his head toward the wall where he's leaning.

Number eight is stenciled to the left of the open front door.

"Oh, crap." I shake my head. "No way. This is a one-bedroom."

"Are you sure?"

"Mia told me specifically. She said she hoped I wouldn't need a bigger space because their two bedrooms were all being used this month."

"I heard that this is the only vacant cabin." Jared steps inside the door. "Come on in, and we'll check it out."

I follow him inside reluctantly. I don't want to get attached to the place when clearly I can't stay here. Because I know Jared. He's not so gentlemanly that he'll offer to leave. Instead, he'll suggest we cohabitate. And cohabitating is the last thing I feel capable of doing with Jared Storm.

"Where's your kitty?" I ask him as we pass through an open-concept living room and small but complete kitchen.

"She's at the main house in Luke's office. Chase is allergic, so it's short-term."

I pull up short when we turn down the narrow hallway to the bedroom and bathroom across from it.

"Definitely a one-bedroom," I say awkwardly as I stare at the king-sized bed with rustic bedframe and multi-colored quilt. "That's all you and your kitty cat."

Jared catches my wrist as I turn to leave. The electric current that passes between us is so intense I suck in a loud breath.

His eyes darken.

Great, so he felt it, too.

It's not like I've never felt any kind of vibe from Jared. I know he finds me attractive. I just also know he finds a lot of women attractive. I'm special to him for what we shared as kids and for the fact that he trusts me when he doesn't really trust anyone. But I'm not naïve enough to think that I'd be any more special to him in the bedroom than the next girl he decides he wants.

I gently detach my wrist from his warm, large hand, and step back. "Come on, J. This isn't an option."

"What isn't an option?"

"Us. In this cabin together."

"Question." He beckons me out to the living room where he takes a seat on the l-shaped couch.

I sit at the other end, as far away from his sexiness as possible.

"Why can't we do this until I find a new place?" he asks me. "We've slept in the same bed together many times before."

"We were kids!" I say.

"We shared a bed as teenagers too," he reminds me.

My face is so hot I feel like I need to jump in the lake. I'm seriously considering it.

"So? That doesn't mean we need to do it as adults also." I realize too late how sexual that sounds coming out of my mouth, and I roll my eyes in frustration.

Jared just winks at me.

"I'm honestly so pissed off at this situation," I say. "I have serious jetlag. You know how I hate to fly." I hold up a lock of my shoulder-length hair. "My hair's a damn mess with all these flyaways. I'm sweaty and dehydrated. I just want to take a nap and then get up and go to a bar for some beers and fried food."

Jared's got a fond smile on his face as I vent. When I finish and take a breath, he leans over to pat my leg.

"Go take a nap, Ash. I'll figure this out while you're asleep. When you wake up, I'm going to take you out for drinks and a good meal."

"Are you sure you can find a place for one of us to live, starting tonight?"

"I'm sure. Right now, I'm going to go check on the cat." He stands up.

"Okay." I stand too.

He steps closer and gives me a gentle kiss on the head.

That was unexpected.

I look up at him. "Thank you."

"Sure." He looks like he wants to say more, but all he does is wave before turning for the door. "Have a good sleep."

As soon as he's gone, I head straight for the divine-looking bed, throw myself under the cozy quilt and cool sheets, and do just that.

CHAPTER FIVE

Jared

I park my truck haphazardly outside the main house of Wild Ranch.

Luke and Declan are grilling on the back porch, and they wave at me as I hop out of the truck and head toward them. They may not be brothers, but the two oldest Wild cousins look so much alike with their tall, muscular builds and dark hair. Yet, Luke's blue eyes and the jagged scar on his cheek, not to mention his cowboy hat, make it obvious which one's the cowboy.

"Your cat is in my office," Luke says as I reach them.

"I'll get her in a minute," I tell him.

"How's the cabin?" Declan asks.

"The cabin itself is fine. But we've got a problem," I say.

Luke offers me a burger, and I accept. Even though I'm going to eat with Ashley later, as a professional athlete, I'm pretty much always hungry.

I bite into my burger and moan. Local, grass-fed beef is so damn good.

"This from one of yours?" I ask in between mouthfuls. I'm

saying it to fuck with him because I already know what the answer will be.

Luke shoots me a look of disbelief. "Of course it is. Where the hell else would we get it?"

One thing I've learned since moving to Montana is that ranchers are particular. My brothers and I didn't grow up with a lot of money, so any food was good food. And beef was beef.

But here at Wild Ranch, produce is either home-grown or comes from their brother, Brayden's, ranch. And the meats? They usually come from their own livestock. Cattle ranchers are competitive as hell, a fact I can relate to and appreciate. After all, I didn't get where I am without one big-ass competitive gene.

"What's the problem?" Luke asks as he finishes at the grill.

I take a seat on the patio couch. Declan joins me, and Luke sits down in the wooden rocking chair across from us.

"I've got myself an unexpected roommate."

Declan raises his eyebrows. "What do you mean?"

"Seems as if your wife also promised cabin eight to someone."

Luke looks over at Declan. "Do you know what the hell he's talking about?"

I see the moment that the realization crosses Declan's face. "No fucking way."

"Yep." I tilt my head toward my truck. "I picked Ashley Hill up at the airport, and Mia's text directions led us straight to cabin eight."

"Fuck." Declan runs a hand down his face. "I forgot Mia had promised Ashley a place here."

Luke curses. "That's a one-bedroom."

I'm well aware of that fact. The other fact is that I can barely keep my hands off Ashley Hill on a normal day. Put us in forced proximity to one another, and I'm going to become a desperate man.

Ashley and I are just friends.

I've been repeating that mantra to myself going on three years now.

Each time I see her, my desire for her grows. I don't know how I made it through our teenage years without making a move on her, but our friendship was too important for me to risk. As a kid, I was downright stupid. Reckless. And I would never have dragged her down with me.

But now that we're adults? My craving for her feels like too much to ignore.

"I'm sorry," Luke is saying, and I drag my thoughts out of the dirt and back to the present moment. "There's literally nothing I can do for the next four weeks. We don't have a single empty space on the ranch with all these damn bloggers. And our cousins are up from Texas, so they're staying at the house—even the couch is filled. In a month, I can set Ashley up in a different cabin. But until then…"

I blow out a breath. "It'll be okay."

Luke narrows his eyes. "Are you sure?"

"Sure. It's just a month, right?"

"You could get an apartment in town that takes pets," Declan suggests with a raised eyebrow.

Yes. I could do that. But the truth is that I don't want to. I love Wild Ranch. And the idea of exploring the ranch with Ashley is too enticing to pass up.

I shrug. "I'll talk to Ashley about it."

"Exactly what is your relationship with Ashley?" Luke asks.

Declan chuckles. "Don't use the r-word around Jared. He's allergic."

I flip him off. "Hey. You're no longer my teammate. You're my boss. So you can't give me shit anymore."

Declan grins. "We're not on the clock right now. So we're not boss and player. We're friends hanging out."

Luke shakes his head. "Hockey players and cowboys aren't as different as I would have thought. You two sound like me and my brothers."

"Plus," Declan says, "as a Wild Kings player, you work for me. And I want to make sure you'll be well-rested for our opener this week. So if your living arrangement is an issue..."

"I'll be fine." I stand up. "I'll go grab the cat, and then I've got to deliver the news to Ashley. She's not going to be happy."

"Good luck!" Declan calls out to me as I head inside the house with Luke. "And remember: Close proximity can be a good thing."

Ha. I know what he's doing. He wants to remind me how he and Mia ended up together. They had some sort of arranged marriage—although he never told me in so many words, and I never came out and asked. It was more of a hunch.

But obviously, all's well that ends well as Declan and Mia are really and truly in love. And living together in a cabin on Wild Ranch apparently cemented their lifetime commitment to one another.

Ashley and I are different, though. We've been friends forever, since before my mother died from cancer when I was just a kid. We slept over at each other's houses since we were young—and in each other's beds when we were teenagers. I always thought—and still do to this day—that she was the most beautiful, kick-ass girl on the planet. That straight auburn hair with the one wavy lock she could never tame—and her hazel eyes with violet flecks always saw right through me. I loved her from the moment we met at recess in elementary school. And despite how much I cared for this girl...

Nothing ever happened.

Because I never deserved her. And I never wanted to disappoint or hurt her. My girl had been through too much pain already in her life. I wouldn't have been able to live with myself if I added to Ashley's pile of shitty relationships. Her family was bad enough.

I dated girls I wasn't friends with. Ones where I didn't know their favorite color or what t-shirt they preferred to sleep in at night.

At one point, I almost caved. Shortly before Dad was murdered, I had a moment of boldness where I considered asking Ash to Prom. She knew it, too. She made it clear she would say yes. Then Dad died, and any risk I was willing to take burned out. Like the light in my eyes.

I was suddenly parentless at seventeen. It's a heavy burden to carry for four boys from the wrong side of town who didn't have a fucking clue how to support themselves. All we had was hockey.

Hockey became not only my goal—it became my obsession. I poured all my grief, all my worries, all my rage into making it to the pros one day.

Going to Prom took a backseat. So did any thoughts I had of being good enough for Ashley.

Here I am, all these years later, and I still don't think I'm good enough for her. But I'm going to be living with her for the next month.

Inhaling her honeysuckle scent, sitting across from her at the breakfast table while we sip our coffees, looking into her hazel eyes with the violet flecks and the bottomless depths of emotion.

That's sweet torture if I've ever heard it.

But it's a torture I can't imagine walking away from. Not without a fight.

CHAPTER SIX

Ashley

It's dark when I wake up. I'm disoriented, and for a moment, I have no clue where I am.

Then it all comes back to me.

Montana.

Cabin.

Jared.

"Oh, God." I pull the covers over my head.

Maybe Jared's already found a solution to our problem.

I lie there quietly for a few more minutes, but my hunger gets the best of me.

I slide out from underneath the soft, silky covers and grab a small bag from one of my suitcases before I make my way into the bathroom across the hall. I splash cold water on my face before looking in the mirror.

I look exactly the way I feel—messy. I'm dehydrated and can't wait for a drink; my hair, normally straight and well-tamed except for one irritating lock, is a frizzy mane around my head. The altitude combined with the long flight has not been kind to my hair or my skin, which is a combination of blotchy and dry.

I finger-comb my hair and pull it back into a ponytail with an elastic band from my bag. Then I brush my teeth and apply clear lip gloss. I rarely wear makeup, and I don't feel like changing things up tonight.

I leave the bathroom and grab my phone, checking my messages as I walk down the short hall.

Emerson texted to welcome me to Montana and ask if I want to meet for coffee later this week. I text her back a *yes*. She's engaged to Max Storm, and I knew her when she lived in New Orleans as a kid. She's kind and sweet and brilliant, and I'm happy to have someone else besides Jared here that I already knew, even if it's been years since Emerson and I hung out.

I keep scrolling through my phone. Winter left me a voice-mail. She and Peyton are my two best friends from home, and Winter and Jared's younger brother, Hunter, are getting married this year.

I smile when I think about it. Peyton's already in a serious relationship, and now Winter's about to become a wife. And not just anyone's wife. A Storm brother's wife. It's hard to fathom.

"Hey."

I look up. Jared's sitting on the couch with only a dim light on in the kitchen.

"Hey."

His eyes warm as he pats the couch cushion next to him. "Come sit."

I freeze as I look at his expression. When he reaches behind him and rubs his neck, I groan. "Crap. You didn't find a solution, did you?"

"Meow!"

I whip around at the sound.

"Oh my gosh!"

I walk over to the kitchen counter where a beautiful gray-and-white tiger-striped cat is sitting like she already owns the place.

"She's gorgeous!" I put out my hand and she sniffs it cautiously. "Can I pet you?"

"Meow!"

I laugh and run my hand over her soft, short fur. "You're so pretty. What's your name?"

"You want to help me figure that out?"

I turn back to Jared, who's grinning from his front-row seat of watching me fall in love with his cat.

"I can see why you were willing to get kicked out of your condo," I tell him as I give the cat one last pet before walking over to sit next to him on the couch. "She's precious."

The kitty jumps off the countertop and settles herself on Jared's lap.

I try not to get sappy.

But watching tough-guy Jared love on a cat is making my heart feel things I've been trying really hard to avoid feeling.

"I can find a new apartment, Ash." His voice is low as he pets the kitty. "Just not tonight."

"But you were looking forward to living on the ranch. I know you were."

"How do you know I didn't come up with a solution?" he says abruptly.

"Because I know you. It was written all over your face—from your pleading eyes to your guilty tone of voice. Plus, you rubbed the back of your neck. You only do that when you're anxious."

"So you know my tells too."

"Of course I do. We spent so many nights together—" I pause but then keep going— "especially at your place growing up whenever my stepdad would get violent."

Jared clenches his jaw. "I'm sorry to say this, but I'm not sorry that fucker's dead."

His words hit my stomach like lead. I can't disagree with him, though. That time in my life is a blur of terror mixed with anger and sadness.

But we survived. Even though I've concealed the truth of that last night from everyone but my mama and the police officer we gave our statement to.

"I'm okay now," I tell him.

"You're better than okay. You're the best."

"Thank you."

"Ash." He turns to face me. "I really will get an apartment. I just need a couple of days."

"I'm fine with you staying here. I can look for an apartment."

"No. You stay." His brown eyes fix on the cat as he says, "So. You want to help me name her?"

I'm a mess right now. Part of me wants to make a happy home with Jared and "our" cat on a ranch, and part of me needs to stay strong about how unrealistic this whole thing is.

But the dreamer side of Ashley Hill wins out.

"Let's try it," I find myself saying.

Jared glances over at me with eyes wide, and I know I've surprised him. In a good way.

"Try what?"

"You. Me. Louise."

"Louise?"

"Our cat. A shout-out to our home state. And we could call her Louie for short."

"Louie." His lips twitch.

"What's funny?" I nudge his leg with my bare foot.

I don't expect him to grab my foot and hold on.

My stomach starts doing cartwheels.

"Nothing."

He lets my foot go, and I exhale.

I'm relieved, not disappointed.

Right.

"I like the name."

"You do?" I can't help but smile.

"I do. It sounds a bit like Liam's daughter, Lulu. Louie's her cousin, right?"

"Her fur cousin."

"Fur cousin."

His eyes lock with mine.

Four beats pass, and the air in the cabin grows uncomfortably thick. Jared's eyes are unfathomably deep with all sorts of emotions, and I can read all of them—pain, longing, sadness, fear, curiosity.

Crap. I'm jetlagged to holy Hell, and this man gets to me on a good day.

I jump up. "Didn't you promise me a meal and some alcohol? I'll grab my purse."

CHAPTER SEVEN

My phone rings just as I enter the bedroom. I shut the door and pick up the call.

"How's Montana, sugar?" Winter asks me before I've even had time to say hello. "Is it beautiful? Peaceful? Do you love your lodging..."

"Jared Storm is my freaking housemate."

"*What?!*"

"Scratch that. He's my roommate. Room—mate," I add for emphasis as all my frustrations from the day bubble to the surface. Winter Allen may be about to become Jared's sister-in-law, but she's been my bestie since we were toddlers, and I know she'll understand.

"Hold up." Winter's tone goes from playful to near-panic. "Jared's your *roommate?*"

"Yes."

"But how? Why? Can't you just kick him out?"

"Not fast enough." I fill her in on how Jared surprised me at the airport and we ended up here. "And he swears it will all be okay and *why don't we just try it?* His cat did me in."

"That sounds like a Storm," Winter murmurs, and I can hear

the sympathy in her voice. "I can understand how you're feeling."

Yes, she can. Winter ended up as Hunter's housemate when she returned home to New Orleans, under a similarly-unplanned situation. Of course, they used to hook up as teenagers, and before long, they were again. All of these thoughts cross my mind, which makes me think of Jared, and now my face feels very hot.

I fan my cheeks with my free hand as I say, rapid-fire, "Not the same relationship between Jared and me. We've always just been friends."

"But you two have something else going on," Winter says. "I don't know exactly what, but we can all see it."

I jump in before she can say more. "It's just too...close quarters here."

"Maybe Jared's right. Trying it isn't the worst idea," Winter says, and I can tell she's decided to change tacks.

"I know where you're going," I say to her. "You want to help, and you're actually encouraging me to follow my feelings."

"Well, it's better than burying your feelings."

"Not in this case."

Winter laughs. "I expect a full report in the morning."

"Not a chance. Nothing is going to happen tonight. Promise."

"How about a text and a photo of your cabin?"

"I'll consider it."

We both laugh.

"I miss you, Win. I'm already homesick."

"Miss you too. Peyton and I went out for drinks tonight. It wasn't the same without you."

The knock on my door makes me jump.

"Be right there!" I call out. "I better go," I say to Winter. "Send Peyton my love."

———

Thirty minutes later, Jared and I sit across from one another at a booth in the back of the Lucky Cowboy bar. We each have a pint of beer and are sharing a plate of chicken wings and fries.

Jared grumbled that I'm bad for his healthy diet, but he didn't fight me very hard when I went ahead and ordered the wings plate for two. I know what he likes, and I know when he needs to let the job go and relax for an evening. His eyes have dark circles under them, and I have yet to learn why.

I glance around the dimly lit bar at the sea of cowboy boots and hats.

"You don't seem to fit in here," I say as I turn back to him.

He grins. "You'd be surprised."

"Would I?" I smile at him. "I doubt that, Storm. You're always surprising me."

"So tell me this." He pops a fry into his mouth, chews, and swallows before continuing. "How come I never knew I liked horseback riding?"

"Because you never tried it," I say. "Duh. We grew up in a city."

"That's true," he says. "But I also used to think I was scared of horses. Scratch that. I *was* scared of horses."

"Because you went on a hay ride with your family in rural Louisiana one time, and a horse bit you." I take a big sip of my beer, and then another.

I peer over the rim of my mug at Jared, who's staring at me.

"What the heck?" I ask him as I put down my mug.

"You know my backstory too well."

"We can still surprise each other," I say without thinking.

Shit. That sounded flirty.

Jared stills, his fry halfway to his mouth and his eyes not leaving mine.

I resist the urge to fan myself for the second time since I arrived in Montana, which is not hot this time of year. But, God, are my cheeks warm.

I left the steaming south, and yet, I feel like I've never been more heated in my life than I have since I landed here.

"Moving on." *Smooth transition, Ash.* "We better eat up. I'm exhausted." Unable to stop myself, I add, "And you look tired yourself, J."

His jaw clenches, and I know I've caught him off guard.

"I've...had some trouble sleeping," he says like it pains him to admit it.

"Really? That's unlike you. You could always sleep through anything."

He nods but doesn't say anything more.

I don't push. I know I'll find out what's going on eventually. It's pretty much law between Jared and me—other than my deep dark story that I've worked like hell to keep from him, everything else in our lives tends to spill out.

I love having someone in my life who never judges me. And if I weren't so filled with my own self-judgment, I'd have told him my dirtiest secret already. Because Jared is the least judgmental person I know.

I rely on that from him. He accepts people where they're at.

"I'm nervous living away from home," I confess.

Jared swallows his bite of chicken. "That's natural."

"I know. Except, nerves aren't really my go-to."

He chuckles. "You're still fearless, Ash. No worries."

"Ha, ha. I'm serious."

He finishes off his chicken wing and raises his beer. "A toast. To you taking a risk and leaving the Big Easy."

"I didn't have much of a choice if I wanted to keep my job. Although it does feel brand-new."

"Because it is brand-new. You'll be doing different things at your job here, right? Wild West Ash," he adds with a wink.

I laugh. "I'm still doing social media, but I'll be in the field as much as I'll be at a desk out here. And being around horses is a dream of mine."

"I remember your posters."

"Oh, God." I laugh. "Those horsey posters on my bedroom ceiling. I was obsessed. And I'd only ridden a horse at summer camp."

"You can ride every day now if you want to."

I do want to. I want to experience Montana. I'd like to throw myself into Wild Ranch and into my job as much as possible.

I raise my beer and we click mugs. "To taking chances."

"To taking chances," he repeats, his brown eyes locking with mine.

I bring the mug to my mouth to break the eye contact.

CHAPTER EIGHT

Jared

I don't want to stop hanging out with Ashley at the Lucky Cowboy. I'm feeling a bit like the name of the bar, and I haven't felt that way in a long time.

My homegirl being in town is like a breath of fresh air sweeping into Montana. I love Missoula, but I do get homesick for New Orleans. I don't focus on it often, and having my twin brother here with me makes it a hell of a lot easier.

But Max is family. Ashley is a whole other kind of energy. And I can't get enough of hanging with her.

However, she's understandably exhausted after her day of travel, and neither of us can put off the inevitable.

I stuck to one beer with dinner, so I drive us back to Wild Ranch while Ashley fights to stay awake in the passenger seat next to me.

"We're home, sleepyhead," I tell her quietly as I park next to our cabin.

I really need to stop saying things like "home" and "our cabin." In a month, I'll be moving out, so the less attached I get to my current living arrangement, the better.

"So," she says in an extra-slow Louisiana drawl as we enter the cabin and both pause in the living room.

"So," I imitate her, enjoying the way the southern sound rolls off my tongue. I haven't tried to get rid of my accent, but it's always more pronounced around people from home.

She huffs out a breath in an attempt to sound irritated, but I know she's trying not to commit to a sleeping decision. Just like I am.

Like she can sense the awkwardness, Louie gets up from her resting place on the couch and wraps her tail around my leg.

"She's hungry," Ashley says as she heads for the kitchen. "I'll fix her up a can of food."

Ten minutes later, the cat is happily eating, and Ashley and I are out of excuses.

"Look." I break the tension. "This is uncomfortable. We both know that. I'll take the couch, and you have the bedroom."

Ashley scans my face. I don't know what she's looking for exactly, but she obviously decides something because she reaches out her hand to me.

"We'll share the bed."

I blink. "What?"

"I thought you'd want to." She blushes. "Whatever. If you don't…"

"I do." I grab her extended hand. "Of course I do. I was just surprised is all."

"Don't overthink it," she tells me as she leads me to the bedroom.

"Never," I promise.

"I just want to make sure you get your proper rest leading up to your opener."

"Of course." I hide my grin.

As soon as we enter the room, Ashley drops my hand and kneels down by her suitcase on the floor. "I'm going to take a quick shower before crashing."

"I'll do the same."

Her hand that's lifting the lid of the suitcase freezes.

"After you," I say hurriedly. "You go first. Of course."

She nods quickly. "Okay. Right. I'll be fast."

"No rush. I'm going to grab my bags out of my truck."

———

Ashley and I aren't kids anymore. We're both adults, and we know better than to make a big deal out of a small thing like sharing a bed.

Plus, we have a third body in the bed.

That's right—Louie joined us shortly after we both showered, and she's currently loudly purring at our feet. She's definitely an icebreaker, that one.

Ashley spends the next five minutes sitting up so she can pet Louie and whisper silly talk to her.

"You're the sweetest kitty in the world, aren't you?"

I laugh. "She's already got you wrapped around her finger."

"Like she doesn't have you." I can hear the smile in her voice.

"I'm not spoiling her," I say immediately.

"Sure you're not. She's already sleeping in your bed. Win told me Hunter would make their kitty sleep separately so he could get a good night of rest during the season. She overrules him a lot, of course."

I chuckle. "Of course. And I'm not as hardcore as Hunt. I don't mind a little nighttime interruption."

That came out way more suggestive than I'd planned.

Ashley's hand on Louie stills, and she ducks her head so I can't see her expression.

"Anyway, I'm not worried," I add quickly.

"Good. Because our kitty is very content right here."

Our kitty.

Why can't we stop with the damn possessives?

"Well, good night," Ashley tells me as she flops onto her back and leans over to turn off her bedside lamp.

"Good night, Ash."

I stay on my back as she shifts onto her side so she's facing away from me.

I wait for her breathing to even out.

But it never comes. And by the sounds of how she's rustling the sheets but trying to be quiet, she's obviously as awake as I am.

After about fifteen minutes, during which I fight like hell to ignore the fact there's a beautiful woman I actually also enjoy talking to a foot away from me, she calls my name softly.

"Yeah?" I say back.

"I had one beer too many at dinner." She giggles.

I smile. "Are you buzzing?"

"A little." Pause. "Remember how I'd climb in through your window?"

"My brothers were never the wiser. Dumb-asses," I say fondly.

"I've missed living near you, J."

"Me too, darling."

"I'm really going to sleep now."

"Okay."

This time, her breathing does even out.

The sound of it relaxes me, and for the first time in fucking forever, I fall asleep without effort.

The light coming in through the cabin window wakes me.

The fragrance of magnolias gets my attention, along with the soft, warm body pressed against my stomach.

I don't know when or how it happened, but Ashley and I are spooning. Last thing I remember, we were saying good night and making sure to keep our physical space.

But shit, I feel good. I slept better than I have in a year. Not a coincidence, obviously, that I'm next to my best friend.

She's still sleeping, and I don't want to wake her, so I stay as still as possible. My body is reacting to her closeness, though, especially one part of me, and I try to subtly shift back from her.

"Hey, Storm." Ashley's voice is husky from sleep, and she rolls out of my arms instantly.

"Hey."

She turns back to look at me. "How the heck did we end up spooning?"

I chuckle. "Old habits die hard?"

Ashley and I cuddled often as teenagers. I don't think I can name another woman I've cuddled with. The irony isn't lost on me since Ash is the only girl I've shared a bed with that I didn't fuck. And yet...

"You soothe me," pops out of my mouth.

She stares at me like I just revealed something big. Her beautiful eyes widen a fraction of an inch, and her pouty lips part.

Meow!

I glance down at the foot of the bed where a gray and white tiger-striped feline is eyeing me.

"You hungry?" I say to Louie. "Food's in the other room."

She jumps off the bed and, with a flick of her tail, sashays out of the bedroom.

I turn back to Ashley. "She seems to be fitting in well. Certainly doesn't lack for confidence."

Ashley smiles, but her attention is on me. She studies my face for several seconds before saying, "So there *is* something going on with you."

"What do you mean?" I ask her.

She reaches over and pats my cheek gently. "You look exhausted, J."

CHAPTER NINE

Ashley

"Like I told you, I've had a little issue with sleep," he says.

I look more closely at Jared's eyes. "Well, your dark circles aren't quite as dark this morning. So what's up with the insomnia?"

"When Declan retired, it was a lot of pressure," he admits. "We were the defending champs, and anything less than a repeat would be a disappointment."

"So you think you were a disappointment last year because you didn't win it all?"

He shrugs.

"J." I take his hand and squeeze it. "What is this really about? Because I'm calling bullshit on the Declan angle. The Jared Storm I know doesn't feel pressure."

"True." He exhales like it pains him to even talk about his feelings.

That's a Storm for you. Their daddy was a good man, but he wasn't big on emotional chats, and their mama died so long ago. The four brothers are great guys, but handling big emotions isn't one of their strengths.

"So what's going on? You know that whatever you tell me won't leave this room."

He squeezes my hand back. "After we won, I felt like I'd reached my dreams. All the ones I'd promised my parents I'd achieve. And when you reach the pinnacle and no one is there to celebrate with you..." He lets go of my hand and flicks it in the air like he's conflicted. "It feels kind of lonely."

My heart breaks. "So a part of you doesn't want to win. Because then you'll feel that loneliness all over again."

"It's psychological warfare," he says. "It's nuts."

"It's not," I say. "It makes sense. I get it."

Jared exhales. "I can't let it continue into this season. I have to show up for my teammates."

"You always show up. For everyone." We lock eyes. "You've always shown up for me. And you'll figure this problem out. I believe in you."

His eyes warm. "I'm glad you're in Montana, Ash. Do you want to go for a ride together before you start your day? I can saddle up two horses in no time."

I smile. "I would love to. Let me just..." I grab my phone off the nightstand and glance at the screen. "Shit. Mia texted and wants to meet me asap. Raincheck on the ride?"

Jared winks. "Anytime, Ash."

My cheeks warm, and I can feel my toes curling underneath the sheets. His brown eyes roam my face before landing on my mouth for a beat too long.

I swallow, and he drags his attention back to my eyes.

"I'll let you get ready," he says as he stands up.

His muscles are on full display underneath his fitted t-shirt and track pants. His messy hair and facial hair just add to his sexiness.

I resist the urge to ask him to stay, and he leaves the bedroom, shutting the door behind him so I'm alone with my lust.

But my pulse is all over the place, and my stomach's flipping with butterflies. Jared's heated gaze could melt an ice storm, which is perfect, given his surname. And as hard as I'm trying to keep a line between us, it already feels tenuous at best.

I'm not sure I even want to resist the sparks between us.

But I can't deal with that now. It's time to get dressed for my first day of work.

———

As the CEO, Mia's Missoula office is epic with floor-to-ceiling windows and a beautiful view of the river below. I'm thrilled with my space, which is directly next to hers and has a sliver of the same view of the outside. I'll be in this office a lot, but I get to spend a part of each day on Wild Ranch. I can't wait for both, and I can feel my creativity growing with each moment I'm in Montana.

"I'm so sorry about the cabin mix-up." Mia widens her eyes in apology as she finishes showing me around the building and leads me back to her office to chat. "My husband and I thought of the same good idea, I guess. Clearly, we should have communicated that to each other."

I wave it off. "You two have a new baby to focus on. I'm sure a lot of other things get forgotten. With good reason."

"I just feel terrible that one of you will have to move."

I suck in a breath. "Well, we're going to try staying there together for the month and see how it goes."

Mia sits down in her chair behind her desk and gestures that I sit across from her. "Are you sure? I know you and Jared are old friends, but I don't want you to feel uncomfortable."

Remembering Jared's heated look this morning as we lay in bed together, I fight not to sound awkward as I stammer out that it's fine.

"How about you come with me to the Lucky Cowboy tonight?" Mia asks me suddenly. "Jamie Beth and Haley are joining me." She laughs. "Declan's on babysitting duty."

"I don't want to intrude."

"You're not. Plus, Haley Laine is your new work colleague, so it would be good for you two to get to know each other better. And Jamie's the best."

I would love a night out with other women.

"That sounds fun." I glance at my phone. "I need to go pick up my car at the leasing office. I'm getting one with all-wheel drive, which will hopefully help me when it snows. Coming from Louisiana, I'm not exactly prepared for that part."

"It will. And I'll take you." Mia stands up. "I can show you around Missoula at the same time."

———

"So, have you and Jared slept together?" Jamie Beth asks me later that night as she, Mia, Haley, and I sit at a booth at the Lucky Cowboy.

"Manners, JB!" Mia says. "You and Ashley aren't close enough yet to ask that personal of a question. And you're even sober!"

Mia's still breastfeeding, and she isn't ready to drink alcohol yet, so she's sipping on a Shirley Temple, and Jamie Beth is joining her. Haley and I are each two beers in.

Haley laughs, her pretty blue eyes sparkling with amusement behind her black cat-eye glasses. "No subtlety, Jamie."

Jamie Beth tugs at her long red hair and groans. "I'm sorry, Ashley. My mouth opens before I can think sometimes."

I wave off her apology. "I don't mind the bluntness. It's a relief in a way. No one from home dares to ask me what exactly is up between Jared and me."

Haley tilts her blond head. "Are you and Jared more than friends?"

"We..." I inhale. "We never were. But there's always been an undercurrent of..."

"Physical attraction?" Haley says breathlessly.

I nod. "I've never wanted to wade into that territory with him."

"I understand," Mia says. "These hockey boys take up a lot of space energetically."

"For sure," I say. "Jared is amazing and wonderful and the best guy, but I know how shitty he is at dating."

"And that scares you?" Jamie Beth asks me.

"Terrifies is more like it." I let out a shaky laugh. "My home life growing up sucked. That's putting it mildly. So I'm not interested in any kind of relationship unless it's top-notch. I want to be treated well. I deserve to be treated well."

"Yes, you do." Mia nods emphatically.

"And you don't think Jared is capable?" Haley asks.

I shrug. "I'm not trying to put him down. I adore him. And he's gorgeous of course. And successful. But I don't think he wants to settle down. And I'm not built for casual."

"I wish Emerson were here tonight," Haley says. "She's so busy opening up her photo studio. But she would probably be a lot more helpful than us since she's engaged to the other Storm twin. And since she now lives with Max and not me..." She pouts before smiling... "I won't get to see her when I go home."

"She's already texted me," I say. "I'll see her soon, I'm sure."

"Have you told Jared any of what you just told us?" Mia wonders.

"Not in so many words. I don't want to ruin our friendship. I couldn't bear to lose him as a friend."

Jamie Beth assesses me for a moment. "And yet, you look sad."

I look at her in surprise. Winter and Peyton are my closest friends from childhood, and they know me so well. Yet, I don't think they've ever noticed that I'm actually sad about Jared. They're too busy trying to uncover the mystery between us. But the truth is simpler than they think it is.

"I am," I admit. "I think I've always been sad about what could never be."

"I'm sorry." Haley pats my hand. "Living together must be extra challenging."

"It will be fine," I say with a confidence I don't feel.

"Let's all go to the game tomorrow night!" Jamie Beth says. "Mia, can you score us tickets?"

Mia laughs. "Of course. You can all sit in the box with me if you want. I'd love the company. Declan will be there, but he'll be busy chatting with the other owners too."

"Jared invited me to come," I say. "He'll be thrilled if I show up. I told him I wasn't sure I could squeeze it in this week."

"Oh, you have to come!" Jamie puts her hands in a prayer pose. "We'll have so much fun."

"Okay," I say with a laugh. "Since you're twisting my arm and all."

We're busy chatting so I'm not looking around at the bar, but the hair on the back of my neck stands up at the same time that Jamie Beth whistles.

I know without turning that Jared's here. I can feel his presence from across a room.

Jamie says in a low tone, "Whoa. Speak of the devil."

"So much for girls' night," Haley mutters. "The Storm twins are about to crash our party in three, two..."

"Hey."

Jared slides into the booth next to me. He puts his arm around me as Max nods his head at me and grins before taking the seat across from us on the other side of Mia.

The twins can change the air in a room. With their matching dark hair and wicked smiles, Jared and Max Storm are too hot for their own good. And yet, as much as they look alike physically, their temperaments are quite different.

Max is reserved where Jared is sociable. Even before he fell in love with Emerson, Max wasn't known to date or even flirt much. Jared will flirt with anyone. I always thought if Max found the right woman, he'd have no problem settling down. Jared? Not so much.

Case in point—Jared's phone buzzes in his pocket. He ignores it. It continues to buzz.

"Aren't you going to look at your text?" I ask him.

"Not important," he says.

"How do you know?" I press, knowing I'm just asking for trouble. "It could be Hunter or Liam."

"It's not," Max says with a hard look at Jared. "We just talked to them on our way here."

Across the booth, Haley's eyes narrow behind her glasses. "So it's a female friend?"

"Define friend," Max says.

Jared glares at Max before removing his arm from around me to pull out his phone and glance at the screen.

"No friend," he says firmly. "An old...acquaintance."

Right. More like someone he used to fuck around with.

"So you're still dating a lot?" I ask, trying to keep the jealousy out of my tone. I think I *almost* succeed.

"Define dating," Max says with a gleam in his dark eyes.

"Fuck off, brother," Jared says to his twin as he and Max engage in one of those silent staredowns I've seen them do their entire lives. Some kind of twin telepathy the rest of us aren't privy to. "I'm not kidding."

"I'm sure you're not," Max says. "But you really think Ashley's naïve to your lifestyle? She's the one who filled me in years ago."

That's true. I was the first who realized just how scared Jared is of intimacy. And one drunken night, I told Max. I was worried. Of course, Max brushed it off, saying all four of the brothers have problems getting close to people. But maybe he listened to me more than he let on.

"You think any of us would get off scot-free in that depart-ment after the way we lost our parents?" Jared counters.

Mr. Storm was murdered while cashing at a convenience store in New Orleans when the boys were teenagers. And years before that, their mom died of cancer. Despite the tragedies, all four guys made the pros in ice hockey. And they've all excelled.

It's a beautiful ending from sad, humble beginnings, but not everything is neat and tidy. Sometimes, underneath all that glitter, there's a mess that has to be tended to.

And the thing is, I get it. I get Jared. Because, underneath my friendly, open vibe, I'm not that different than he is. A work in progress who has a hell of a time with trust.

"So what are you two doing out?" Mia asks in an effort to break the awkwardness.

"Emmy's working late," Max says. "I told her I'd pick her up some food, and then this guy called. So here we are. I think my brother's got some nerves about our opener tomorrow night."

He says it without a trace of humor, and I can't tell if he's messing with Jared or being serious.

"We're not drinking," Jared says when Jamie Beth signals to the waiter. "Just water."

He brushes my shoulder with his own. "How was day one at work?"

I smile over at Mia and Haley. "Great. My boss and coworker couldn't be kinder."

"Good." Jared lowers his head and whispers into my ear, "I have an idea for later. Something fun."

I nod, but inside me, the butterflies soar. Jared's tone is flirty and far too interested. He's always interested in me—but as a *person*. Not as a woman.

Yet, ever since I landed in Montana, his interest meter has wandered into sexual territory.

My hopeful high crashes down seconds later when his phone buzzes again. He silences it immediately.

It buzzes again.

"For Christ's sake," he mutters as he looks at the screen and then swipes it. "I'm silencing it," he tells me.

"Don't do it on my account," I say.

"Of course I'm doing it on your account," he says in my ear.

I turn my head so I can lock eyes with him. "Is that so?"

"Yes."

His eyes flash with a fleeting emotion I can't identify before he says in a low tone only meant for me to hear, "Let's talk later."

With no idea what he's getting at, I simply nod and turn back to the rest of the group.

For the next hour, we all chat amicably about casual things. Hockey, horses, and the unusually warm fall weather in Missoula this year. I finish a third beer, and I'm feeling sleepier than I am buzzed. The time change is definitely affecting me. It's not even nine o'clock.

"You tired?" Jared murmurs.

"Yeah."

"I'll take you home whenever you're ready. I need to turn in early myself."

"We should feed Louie too."

"We should."

I catch eyes with him, and we share a smile before I turn back to the rest of the group.

Across from us, Max shifts his gaze from Jared to me. When I catch his eyes, he gives the barest hint of a smirk before turning to ask Jared a hockey-related question.

"The temperature in this booth sure went up a notch when the boys arrived," Jamie Beth murmurs on my other side. "One boy in particular."

"Not because of me," I say back to her. "I'm just minding my own business."

"Catching up with an old friend," she says like she knows exactly how to continue the narrative I want to stick to.

"Yes," I say gratefully. "No biggie."

"Don't you hate when someone you know isn't right for you turns your insides out?" she says like she knows.

I turn to her in surprise. "Do you have a similar situation?"

"Not really. Well, let's just say I know what it feels like to have a nuclear attraction to someone that I have no intention of dating."

"Ah." I glance at her face, which is half-hidden by her gorgeous red hair, and I catch the hint of a blush on her cheeks. "It's not a Storm brother, is it?"

She breaks into laughter. "Definitely not. I don't go for hockey guys. I barely understand the sport. I'm more of a cowboy girl. Despite my absolute best efforts not to be."

I silently wonder who the cowboy is that Jamie Beth unwillingly desires and if his last name is Wild.

Before I can decide whether or not I'm drunk enough to ask her something so private, Haley announces she needs to use the restroom.

"I forget where it is," she says with a giggle.

Everyone laughs, but I tell her I need to go too, so we make our way through the bar together.

After going into separate stalls, we stand next to one another at the sinks and wash our hands.

"You should say something to him," Haley says to me with a confident nod. "About your conflicted feelings."

"What?" I say. "To Jared?"

"Uh-huh." She takes off her glasses to clean them, and I marvel at how crystal blue her eyes are.

"Why?" I ask her curiously. "Why would I say something?"

Haley's state of inebriation appears to be making her more open. "Because you want to."

I stare at her. "Do I though?"

"Don't you?" She stares back at me. "I get it. Jared's a lot to handle. And I know you and I are just getting to know each other, but I have a feeling you're definitely strong enough. And maybe you need a man who stands tall on his own. Even though it's scary."

I swallow. "That's always been my weakness. Which is why I make sure to stay single."

Haley laughs. "I'm the same. I seem to only be attracted to

the exact kind of men who would turn my world upside down. And I love my career and my calm, peaceful life. So I choose not to rock the boat. But you? You look like you need to be rocked. No pun intended."

"That may be," I say. "But you heard Jared's phone ping. He's not a one-woman man. And that's a line I won't cross."

CHAPTER TEN

"You must be tired, Ashley," Mia says when Haley and I return to the booth. "It's so much later in New Orleans."

"I am," I admit. "I may call it a night."

"I'll take you home." Jared stands up.

We say our goodbyes, and Max leaves with us.

Once the three of us reach Jared's truck in the back parking lot, Max insists on sitting in the back.

"I'm getting out before you," he says as he hops in. "My place isn't too far from here."

Jared opens the passenger door for me and closes it softly after I'm safely inside. I put on my seat belt and spend the next ten minutes laughing as the guys recant stories from our past, like when Jared stole Max's clothes from his locker and Max chased his brother across the school grounds completely naked.

Jared and Max together are fun. And being with two guys from home is comforting when I just moved so far away.

We stop so Max can pick up take-out from a Thai restaurant for him and Emerson and then continue toward their condo.

"How is Emerson?" I ask Max as Jared pulls into an underground parking garage beneath a beautiful high-rise.

"She's amazing."

I can hear the love in his voice, and I smile.

"I'm happy for you," I tell him. "You two had a good time in Yellowstone this summer?"

"The best. It's good to be back in Missoula, though. This feels like home to us." He pats my shoulder. "Hopefully you'll find love here too, Ash."

I startle.

But Jared pulls the car to a stop in front of an elevator bank, and Max jumps out.

"See you tomorrow, J. Hope to see you soon, Ashley." He waves and shuts his door behind him.

I watch him walk toward the elevator bank and disappear inside.

"He seems like he's doing well." I turn to Jared, who's watching me. "This is the happiest I've seen him."

"I know." Jared chuckles. "Who could have predicted my two younger brothers would be in relationships and Liam and I would be single as hell?"

"*Two* younger brothers? I get that Hunter is the baby of the family. But Max and you are twins!"

"He was born fifteen minutes after me. He's younger."

I laugh.

"Competitive much?"

"Always."

He's smiling as he turns the wheel and we start driving through the parking garage.

Neither of us speaks until we've exited the garage and are headed down the highway.

"So what's your big plan for tonight?" I ask him.

He just smiles. That real genuine Jared smile he only reserves for those in his inner circle.

And I melt. My heart is normally so guarded. I have good reason after the way my stepdad treated my mom. So I don't let my guard down for just anyone.

But with Jared, I've always been a sucker for that smile of his.

"You're so damn cute," I mutter.

"What's that, Hill?" His smile shifts to the cocky kind, the one I always run from. "Did you just say I'm cute?"

"Like a little boy," I snap. "You're cute the way a kid is when you want to pat their head and tell them 'good job' for doing so well at something."

He shakes his head with a chuckle. "You're a terrible liar."

"What do you mean?" I shift to face his profile as he drives. "How am I lying right now?"

"You find me attractive, and you wish you didn't," he says simply. "So you make up stories in your head about looking at me like a little boy. When sometimes—like right now—you really look at me like you want to rip off my clothes."

I suck air in through my gritted teeth. "Do not," I force out.

"Do too," he counters. "You were looking at me like that at the bar too. After a couple of drinks, you're worse at hiding it."

Oh shit, I hate how well he knows me.

"You drive me mad." I turn back and stare out the windshield at the city lights passing us by.

"Speaking of," he says casually. "I'm not seeing anyone while you and I are living together."

CHAPTER ELEVEN

I whip my head over to him again. "What do you mean? You and I aren't sleeping together for real."

"I know that. But I still feel like I'd be cheating on you if I went on a date with another woman while you and I are sharing a bed."

"Oh." That's sweet of him, but still... "I don't know. It feels awkward."

"Why?"

"Because it's us. We shared a bed as teenagers, and you still went on dates. So did I."

"I guess I feel like this time is different."

There go those butterflies swooping through my stomach again. I may as well call them Jared butterflies since he's the only man that can affect me this way.

"Fine," I say noncommittally.

"Fine? So you agree?"

"Sure. I won't see anyone else either while we're sharing the cabin."

"Okay."

Jared puts on his blinker, and we take the next exit.

And within a minute, we're in blissful darkness. The town of

Wilcox is small and quiet, and I love that Wild Ranch is close to the city but feels so separate from it.

"It's so still," I whisper.

Jared turns onto the road that I now recognize leads to the ranch.

"It is," he agrees. "Feels like there are more animals than people out here sometimes."

We lapse back into silence as Jared takes the long winding road lined by pine trees. Instead of turning left toward our cabin, though, he hangs a right.

"Where are we going?" I ask him as I cover a yawn.

He reaches over and pats my leg, letting his hand linger just long enough that I feel the heat of his palm through my jeans.

"This will be quick. But I think you'll appreciate it."

We drive for a few minutes more with the road climbing the whole way. All I see is blackness when Jared stops the car and gestures to me to get out.

"You want to take a look?" He's already opening his door.

I shrug and follow suit.

Once I've stepped outside and shut the door behind me, I freeze.

"It's pitch dark," I say. *And I hate the dark.*

"I'm coming over to you now." I feel him next to me. "You're okay. Breathe."

"I can't even see my own hand in front of my face."

I wave it in front of me. Nothing.

I clutch at Jared's arm. "I need to go back in the truck."

"Hold up, Ash. I've got a flashlight app."

I'm still clutching his arm when light emanates from his phone, and he points it so that I can see a wooden bench surrounded by low-lying bushes a few feet away. Even though we're clearly at the top of a hill, the area around the bench is flat. Prairie grass covers the ground.

"I thought we were like at the edge of a cliff," I say. "This is much better than that."

"There's no overhang here. The road just continues around in a loop and then back down to the ranch house. If you walk through the brush over there—" He points his phone straight away—"you could find the cliff's edge, but it's a ways from here."

"How high are we?"

"About six thousand feet. I wanted to bring you here so we can enjoy the night sky together. Remember how we used to climb onto my roof as kids and wish on stars?"

I get choked up and can't answer him. Like he knows, he just takes my hand and leads me over to the bench. Once we're seated, he says, "Is it okay if I turn off the flashlight?"

I squeeze his hand back in response.

Darkness hits me in the face first. That same darkness I felt when I stepped out of Jared's truck a few minutes ago.

"It's scary," I whisper into the air. "So black."

"Keep looking," he whispers back. "Wait for the light."

I squint, feeling like I'm trying to force something that isn't there. The only sounds are nature's—an owl hooting, crickets chirping, and the wind blowing. I shiver in my lightweight jacket.

"Cold?" Jared's arm comes around my shoulders.

"Thank you."

I relax into his side and keep looking into the blackness. And then, I see the stars.

Hundreds of them litter the sky. Gorgeous, bright stars, not masked by city lights or any human intervention.

"Wow," I breathe out.

"Amazing, isn't it?"

"It's a different sky than we grew up with, J."

"Yeah, you can't find this in a city."

"Do you make wishes here?"

"I've only been up here one time. And it was actually by mistake. I took a wrong turn trying to leave the ranch and got so fucking lost. That's when I realized just how big the Wild property is."

"Were you nervous being out by yourself? What if an animal attacked you?"

"Then I may not be here enjoying this view with you. But I was fine. I try not to live in what-ifs."

For me, the darkness brings back memories I don't like to think about. Jared is well aware of my fear of the dark.

"Why did you bring me here?" I ask him.

"Because." He hesitates before continuing. "I want you to find the light in your dark past, Ash. I want that for myself too, I suppose. But you deserve it more than anyone I know."

"You deserve it too, J." I lean my head on his shoulder. "All those stars up there are ours for the taking."

"That's right."

"You're already a star, though." I smile proudly. "You've made your way out of the dark. And I have too, in my own way."

"Yes, you have. But I feel like you're holding onto something, something that's keeping you from fully embracing your present."

He really can see right through me sometimes. It's both unnerving and a turn-on.

"Am I right?"

"What if you are?" I ask him in a soft tone that belies my defensiveness. "What if there's nothing I can do about it?"

"See, I don't believe that. Whatever it is, you can let it go."

"But why should I try?"

"Because you deserve to."

I raise my head off his shoulder and gaze out at the galaxy of constellations like I can become one of them. Maybe if I could, I wouldn't carry around this guilt with me, a guilt that doesn't feel healthy but that has become such a part of me I no longer know who I am without it.

Killing my stepfather wasn't exactly on my list of plans, and while I may not have done so on purpose, the role I did play is something that forever haunts me.

I open my mouth to tell Jared everything. But three beers

weren't enough to loosen my tongue on the only real secret I've ever kept from him. I shut my mouth and resist any urge I have to confess or—even worse—act on the impossible desire I have to kiss him.

Out here in the middle of nowhere, it would be so easy to press my lips to his. I can feel the heat of his body against mine, and I can hear every breath he takes.

"I feel safe with you," I say out loud.

His breath hitches. It's subtle, but with the stillness of the night around us, I hear it.

"You sound surprised," I say. "But you already knew that."

"I did. But it means a lot to me that you do. It's something I'll never take for granted, Ash. You've always had more faith in me than anyone."

"Your family has faith in you."

"I know. But it's different with you." I feel him hesitate like he's going to say more, but he doesn't.

And that's for the best. Whatever he was going to say, it had the potential to lead us into dangerous territory. I'm not his sibling. I'm his friend. A friendship that can morph into more if we're not careful.

Especially since I'm sharing a bed with him.

Time to create some necessary distance, Ash.

I shift forward and slip out from under Jared's arm.

"I'm thankful you brought me here tonight, but I think I'm ready to go."

He brushes a light kiss to my temple. "Let's go home."

CHAPTER TWELVE

Jared

Here comes the part of the day I'm starting to both dread and crave.

Sleeping next to Ashley and pretending it's no big deal is next to impossible.

But I'm doing my best to handle it.

I'm learning that having a third body in the bed helps. Louie is a good distraction, and she likes to sleep at the foot of the bed between mine and Ashley's feet. Any way to put distance between me and the woman lying next to me is a good thing. My body wants nothing more than her on top of me so I can do all the dirty things I'm fantasizing about. Instead, I keep my hands to myself and don't move.

Grappling for a way to bring normalcy to the cloud of sexual tension in the room, I break the silence.

"Did you have fun tonight?" I ask her as we lie motionless on our backs.

I'm as far away from her as possible without falling off the bed, and she's the same on her side.

"I did. Mia was so nice to invite me out."

"I'm sure you miss Win and Peyton."

"I do. But Winter was in New York for so long that we got used to staying close by phone. And Peyton travels a lot."

"I've found when the people in our life really matter to us, distance doesn't hurt the relationship. Max and I are still just as tight with Liam and Hunt despite us living miles away."

"It's a small miracle that the four of you are only on two different teams rather than four," she says.

"True. God willing it worked out that way."

A short silence hits the room.

Until Ashley breaks it. "I do have something to tell you, J."

"I know. You have for a long time."

"You're right." Pause. "How do you know that?"

I can hear the surprise in her voice.

"You've opened your mouth and then closed it a number of times over the years. Like you were holding onto the world's biggest secret and at the same time were desperate to tell someone. I always figured you'd told Winter and Peyton."

"Nope."

I stare up at the ceiling that's just visible in the dark room. "Have you told anyone?"

"My mom knows. But we act like..."

She trails off, but I get her point. Her mom isn't a bad person, but she never would have been nominated for world's greatest mother. And making sure her daughter was okay emotionally wasn't high on her list of concerns.

"Ash." I say her name more gently than I think I ever have. "I'm all for keeping things to myself too, but when something is weighing on you heavily? That's probably not healthy."

"I know it's not. But I can't share it with you when I'm buzzing."

"I agree. Let's talk when we're both sober. Tomorrow?"

I can hear her shaky inhale before she says, "Okay. Good night."

"Good night, Ash."

Ashley

Jared's still sleeping when I wake up the next morning. His first game is tonight, and I don't want to disturb his rest, so I slip out of bed quietly.

Louie follows me into the kitchen.

I spend a few minutes loving up on her with pets and kisses, and then I prepare her breakfast and clean her litter box before getting ready for my second day of work.

After showing me around the corporate headquarters yesterday, Mia asked me to meet her at the main house of Wild Ranch this morning. That's a much shorter commute, and I enjoy the walk to the stables. It's cool out this morning, and I'm glad I wore a warm jacket.

Mia shows me around the barn, and I enjoy petting a few of the horses. I take a few quick photos for my daily social media post while Mia fills me in on what she's looking for.

"Haley was in charge of our socials all last year," she explains. "But once our foundation grew larger, we needed more help. So Haley is focusing on the sales side of marketing now. Which means you'll have a lot of freedom to do what you think is best for growing the foundation even more, and you'll still have Haley to turn to for support."

"That's great. I'm looking forward to it. And I adore horses. It's part of the job I'm most looking forward to—spending time with them."

We're still chatting when the barn door swings open.

"Good morning, ladies."

Three hot-as-hell cowboys stride into the barn, and Mia introduces me to the Wild Brothers.

Luke remembers me from when I was in Montana last year, and I certainly remember him. He's dark-haired and built; the scar on his right cheek adds to his intimidation factor, and I get the feeling he likes it that way. His twin brothers, Chase and Cooper, are blond and full of mischief.

All three guys are wearing worn blue jeans, flannel shirts, and cowboy boots.

"You don't look dressed for a ranch," Chase teases me.

I laugh as I look down at my sneakers and parka. "I've got jeans on, though. Does that count?"

"That definitely counts," Cooper says with a grin. "You'll pick up the rest in no time."

"You should have Jared take you shopping for boots," Luke says dryly.

I roll my eyes. "I don't think Jared ever goes inside a store of any kind unless forced."

"What makes you say that?"

I whip around and look up into the amused eyes of my new roommate.

Roommate.

I shake my head. I still can't believe that word applies to Jared and me.

"Morning." Jared's dark eyes fix only on me.

His hair is messily sexy.

He's dressed casually.

So. Very. Casually.

Black jacket. Blue jeans. Cowboy boots.

Jared Storm wears cowboy boots.

And I am totally here for it.

"I like your boots," I say to him. "Did you actually go shopping?"

He smirks. "I did. That's how I get clothes and shoes to wear."

"Ha ha." I stick out my tongue at him.

He reaches out and tugs at a loose strand of my hair, the only piece not pulled back into a low ponytail. I call it my rebel lock of hair, the one that never behaves. It's always been a favorite thing of Jared's to tease me about it.

I brush his hand away. "Don't be annoying."

"I'm always annoying."

"Not always."

"No?" His tone changes from teasing to flirty.

I freeze, remembering we aren't alone in the barn.

And the awareness that everyone has been watching and listening to us flirt hits me.

Luke clears his throat. "Why don't you two go on a trail ride together? The horses need to be exercised."

"Jared has a game tonight, so..." I begin.

"I'm fine to go on a light ride. I'll take it easy."

"I need to work," is my next excuse.

"No problem," Mia says with a smile. "Since you're going to be doing a lot with our social media accounts, getting to know the horses is essential. I want them to trust you so you can take photos and videos freely. And what better way than a ride?"

"I don't want to take time off work when I'm just starting." That's excuse number three, and I'm not sure I have a fourth up my sleeve.

"This will be work," Mia says. "You need to get to know Wild Ranch."

"I can go later," I say to her. "Maybe with you." *Or alone.*

Okay, so it turns out I did have another excuse. But I'm pretty sure I'm out of them now.

"Jared will be a great guide," Mia says immediately. "I don't have time to show you around the property today, and I don't want you to get lost."

She didn't sound too worried about me getting lost a few minutes earlier, but I don't call her out on her unsubtle attempt at matchmaking. I was guilty of the same thing when Winter and Hunter were trying to avoid admitting what the rest of us had seen all along—they were meant for each other.

Jared and I aren't them, though, and as he and Luke bicker over what horse is best for me to ride, I remind myself of that fact.

"Bossy boys," Mia murmurs next to me, and I hear the amusement in her voice.

"No kidding. Is your husband this bossy?"

"I think it's a toss-up between me and Declan as to who likes to be in charge more," she says with a laugh.

She reaches onto the shelf filled with helmets. "Let's get the right fit."

A short while later, after we wave good-bye to Mia and the Wilds, Duchess and I follow Jared on his horse, a gorgeous chestnut gelding named Boo, across the gravel area outside the barn and across the prairie grass to the forested meadow beyond.

We ride at a slow gait and in silence for a while as I adjust to being on a horse again for the first time since I took riding lessons at church camp in Louisiana for a few summers. When we reach the edge of the forest, the path narrows.

"We'll have to go single file for a short while to get to the prairie. Do you want me to go ahead?" Jared asks me, breaking the quiet stillness.

"Sure."

Duchess and I follow him and Boo along the path covered with pine needles. The sun is peeking through the tall trees, and I inhale, breathing in the incredible scent of pine trees and mountain air.

The silence is therapeutic. I can actually hear the light breeze blowing through the trees around us, along with birds chirping and leaves rustling. The lack of man-made sounds—no voices or vehicles, or construction—relaxes me.

Growing up, my home life was never peaceful. The yelling, the glasses breaking, the slamming doors—all of it was far too frequent. The police were called more than once, but my mom always covered for the terror that was my stepfather. Nights were the worst, which explains my fear of the dark, but Aaron could be drunk at any time of day. He'd come home once the bar of his choosing cut him off, and I'd hide in my bedroom with my stomach in knots as I heard him stomp around. He'd find my mother, and the shouting started soon after.

Our home only got quiet when my stepfather finally passed out, and Mama and I would whisper so we wouldn't wake him.

Loud or quiet, my home life was never stress-free.

I always knew I carried trauma from my childhood, but I didn't realize that I truly didn't know what it felt like not to feel constantly anxious. Even at a lower level as an adult, I've always felt on edge like the next moment something in my world may explode.

Until now.

"I'm already glad I came here," I say out loud.

As we come out of the thicker forest area and into the prairie, the path widens, and Jared slows down so we can ride alongside each other.

"Even though you've got a surprise roommate?" he asks me.

"Even so." I take a deep breath. "Having a friend from home here isn't so bad."

"Yeah?"

"Yeah." I try to steal a glance over at him, but he's already looking at me.

By the heat that fills my face, I know I'm furiously blushing.

My life is not a fairytale, and it's certainly not a "boy meets girl as kids and they end up together forever" kind of story. Jared's phone exploding the entire time we were at the bar last night cleared that temptation right out of my brain.

I just need to make sure I don't forget my brain whenever I'm alone with him. Especially in bed, because every night we go to sleep in the same room is harder and harder. I just need to keep in mind how different we are in terms of what we're wanting.

I want a relationship.

Jared doesn't.

Sometimes, though, like right now with the sweet-smelling

Montana air and the warm sunshine hitting my face as I stare at Jared, it's easy to forget we want different things.

"Ash..." He says my name quietly but in a way that goes straight to my core.

"Yeah?" I lean closer to him.

I'm still leaning when Duchess suddenly bolts.

I have no choice but to grab onto the reins and hang on for dear life.

CHAPTER THIRTEEN

Jared

Shit.

Duchess just freaking *took off* from a calm walk to a full-out gallop.

I'm by no means a skilled rider, but I don't even think—I just urge Boo into a gallop, and we take off after Duchess.

But I'm swallowing my worry as I urge Boo onward.

Ashley is a decent rider, but she doesn't know the ranch, and she's not experienced on trails. And she hasn't ridden in forever.

Duchess disappears over the hill, taking Ashley with her.

My pulse beats in my head.

I can't lose her.

———

Ashley

Duchess flies across the prairie, and I call out to her to slow down.

She doesn't slow, and for a few seconds, I can focus on nothing but the feeling of the wind blowing in my face and the sweet smell of cedar as we soar along the trail. The blood pounds in my ears, and I grip the saddle horn with one hand and the reins with the other.

"Duchess! Whoa, whoa, girl!"

We round another corner, and I see the stream up ahead, and Duchess slows down.

When I'm finally able to bring her back to a walk, Jared rides up next to me on Boo. I pull up to a halt and take a second to catch my breath.

Duchess's unexpected run across the prairie—with me on her back—was exhilarating, but it was also terrifying.

"Ashley." Jared's voice is rough, and he's out of breath.

As am I. I take a second to inhale and then let it out before I say, "Hi."

"You okay?" he asks, and I hear the concern in his tone.

"I'm fine. You don't have to..." I turn my head to face him. Something about his expression breaks my heart. My guard drops on the spot.

Jared's eyes are filled with fear. Panic, really.

"Hey." I reach out and take his hand, which is shaking. "I'm okay. I know how to ride, J."

"I know you do. I also know it's been a while. And she just took off on you. She got spooked."

She's not the only one. Jared looks like he's seen a ghost.

"I'm not going anywhere," I say gently. "I'm safe."

He takes a deep breath, and his expression shifts from fear to relief. "I'm glad you're okay. I couldn't take it if anything ever happened to you."

Our eyes lock, and something changes between us. I don't understand exactly what, but my stomach does cartwheels, and I clutch the reins even tighter.

"Let's..." The word catches in Jared's throat and he coughs. "Let's take a break."

"Good idea."

He means the riding, but I'd also like to take a break from whatever the hell is suddenly going on between us. Because the rise in temperature is alarming. My body is on board with this change in energy, but my brain is most definitely not.

We dismount and loop our horses' reins over the large branches nearby before sitting down at the base of a stand of pine trees.

Jared stretches his legs out before him and crosses them at the ankles. Something about that simple gesture gets my attention. My already-heated body gets hotter, and I find myself staring at Jared's muscled legs. Even with the jeans covering him, it's obvious the man is in phenomenal shape.

I swallow, searching for a way to take my focus off of my nuclear attraction to him.

"Don't you have to get ready for the game?"

"I'll leave for the arena after lunch." He glances at me. "I told you that earlier."

"Oh." I swallow again. "Right. Yeah. I remember now."

He chuckles. "You seem distracted."

"Do I?"

"You do."

That's because you're so damn hot and I am having one hell of a time denying my attraction to you.

"It's pretty warm out," I say lamely. "The sun is so bright."

"Altitude can definitely make the sun feel stronger, but it's also unusually warm for Montana." He bumps my shoulder with his own. "If you have time, I'll bring you by the best place to get blueberry muffins."

I gasp. "I love blueberry muffins!"

He's grinning. "That's why I want to take you there. This place could become your new go-to."

"Like that café we found in New Orleans when we were kids? La..."

"La Dulce," he finishes for me.

I clap my hands. "That place was the best. I was so sad when they left the city because the owners moved back to Texas. I think I've missed having a place ever since."

"You've had other 'places' over the years, I'm sure."

"Not like that one. That one was special because it was..." I cut off.

But Jared finishes my thought once again. "Ours."

"It was." I lean my head on his shoulder.

"Ashley."

"Yeah?" I know where he's going with this. And yet, I'm strangely no longer afraid.

"Tell me."

I stare out at the gorgeous prairie and take a deep breath of the mountain air before I confess my darkest secret.

"I killed my stepfather."

CHAPTER FOURTEEN

The words tumble out of me with no hesitation, no delay.

And once the truth is out, I feel stripped bare. Like I could be destroyed by the slightest breeze.

Jared's arm goes around my waist. "That's not true."

"It's absolutely true!" I sit up straight.

"He died in a fire started by a space heater. You and your mom were lucky you weren't home at the time."

"I left the heater on and forgot to turn it off," I whispered.

Jared's eyes flash with surprise. "Your mom told me Aaron left it on."

"I told her it was me, though." I close my eyes briefly, feeling the hot shame envelop me. "She didn't believe me, so she begged me not to tell the police. But I knew I had to."

"What did they say?"

"That's the thing. I went to the police and tried to confess, but the officer on duty cut me off and told me all the reports had been filed. He wouldn't take my statement. I think he did it to protect me because I was a minor."

"And the police had been to your house numerous times on account of Aaron. Everyone despised the way he treated your mother."

"Yes. Nobody felt sorry for Aaron, that's for sure."

"Did you see the final report?"

"Yes. It didn't mention the location of the heater. Obviously, the officer omitted that detail for my benefit. I haven't been able to forgive myself though. And I've been too ashamed to tell anyone since."

"So it's been eating away at you."

"Yes."

Jared gazes past me into the distance like he's deep in thought. "Are you sure?"

His question catches me off-guard.

"Sure of what?"

"Are you certain you left the heater on?"

"Of course I'm sure," I snap. "I always used the heater in my bedroom, remember?"

"I do."

"And that night, I was rushing because I was anxious to get Mom out of there before Aaron could..." I trail off, but I don't need to continue for Jared to know where I'm going with that sentence.

Aaron hit Mom a lot. Enough that I had to call the cops more than once. Enough that I used to fantasize about him disappearing.

"Anyway, the heater was in my bedroom. I thought I turned it off. I could have sworn that I did, actually. But obviously, I didn't, or the fire wouldn't have gotten started."

"What started it?" Jared pushes me. "The heater must have been close to something flammable, right?"

"The curtains."

I recall the way my stomach dropped when Mom and I went to the station and overheard the desk clerk say that "curtains and space heater" were the cause.

"You always kept the heater far away from the curtains whenever I was over."

It's like Jared's speaking out loud all my arguments when I heard what happened. And yet...the cause of death is undeniable.

"I did, but I had moved it out of my way when I was getting changed, so it was closer to the window than normal." I strain to remember that moment in my mind, but it's blurry like it's been ever since that night. "And then Mama and I left."

"And you never went back inside after the fire was put out," Jared says like he's recounting the moment right along with me.

"Right. Everything of value was destroyed, and Mama and I just wanted a fresh start. It was devastating to lose my childhood mementos, but losing Aaron was a relief."

"It was." Jared shifts and unexpectedly takes my chin in his hand.

He studies my face, and I warm under his gaze.

"What?" I ask him defensively. "What are you searching for?"

"I hate that you feel torn up about that night," he says, his dark eyes filled with emotion. "We called it your reset night—for you and your mom to start over with no one terrifying you on a daily basis."

"I know. And it was." I sigh. "Most of life isn't black and white, J. It's filled with gray. So while I felt tremendous relief that Aaron was out of our lives, I couldn't shake the fact that I killed him."

The memory is so strong I feel like I'm back there in my childhood home with the smell of my stepdad's stale cigarettes and the scent of whiskey permeating the living room where he always camped out whenever he wasn't at a bar. From that room, he could see anyone coming and going, just the way he liked it.

He was hitting Mom a lot that evening. I knew better than to get in the middle. She'd warned me endless times to stay out of it. She was protecting me, but I wanted to protect her.

So when Aaron stumbled to the bathroom, I left my bedroom and, for the first time in my life, convinced Mom to leave for a bit. She always stayed, no matter how rough he got, and no matter how much I begged. And when he'd reach for me...she'd just tell me to run.

So I would, straight to Jared's. All night, I'd pray she'd still be there when I returned home the next morning. By the next day, Aaron would be sober, and he didn't hit her when he wasn't drunk. So the cycle continued throughout my childhood. My dad had left when I was a baby, and Aaron was the only father figure I'd ever known.

Sometimes, I called the cops, but that never ended well. Mama would always cover for Aaron, every single time, and I worried he'd be rougher with her after they left than if they never came at all.

But that night, her eyes were desperate, and she let me lead her to the door. I took away Aaron's whiskey, replaced it with water, and put it next to the chair he was about to fall into.

Then, without a backward glance, my mother and I walked out of our house, unknowingly for the last time.

"She was hurting when we drove to the diner." I flash back to the memory, the images as strong as if it were yesterday. "Her arms were bruised. She looked over at me, and she said she wished we could leave him. Finally. I'd been waiting forever for her to be ready. But she was afraid he'd never stop looking for her. She worried I'd be in danger too." I suck in a sob. "And I..."

"You what?" Jared's voice is so gentle, so soft, I can barely hear him.

"I prayed—I actually *prayed*—to God to make Aaron disappear." I remember that night in my dreams—the nightmare of all nightmares because it was actually real life. "The fact that my prayer was answered...it was a human life."

"He doesn't deserve to be called human," Jared says with raw anger.

"But he was. We all are." I ball my hands into fists. "And yet, when I looked at my mama and realized how much she wanted to finally be free of him, I prayed. It was like I saw a whole new reality for her if he was no longer on this earth."

"And she deserved that. So did you," Jared says. "Darling, you were seventeen years old trying to make the best of a shit situation. You didn't kill anyone, do you hear me? No matter what happened with the heater..."

"Karma," I say simply.

"No." He knows where I'm going, and he cuts me off. "Not karma. Not in this case."

"Yes." I pull at the ends of my hair in frustration. "I wanted him dead. I sometimes wonder if, maybe subconsciously, I left the heater on purpo..."

"Not true." Jared's tone is fiercely adamant. "Don't go there. It's not true."

I stare at him. "I was sure you would look at me differently for this. I blame myself for his death. I always have."

"I'm sorry you've held onto the guilt. But it's not your fault."

"I know I didn't commit arson. Nothing was premeditated. But the truth is that...I felt relief." I choke on those last three words. Laced with guilt and indecisiveness.

"You put your mother first. Like you always did. And that fucked you up on more than one occasion. I remember how she would choose him over you. Over and over, she put you in impossible situations."

"I know she did. That's why I spent so many nights hiding in your bed."

"So maybe this one time—you put yourself first."

I clench my jaw.

"Maybe that's why you feel so guilty. Because you actually chose yourself when you persuaded her to leave with you. She had never left him before. Not one time. Not even for dinner."

I swallow hard. "You make a lot of sense."

He runs his hand through his hair, his mouth pursed in concentration.

I know that look. That's Jared's expression when he's thinking over something. Something most of us don't think of.

He can go deep on a topic and come up with things I could never think of.

"What?" I ask him suspiciously.

He blinks once, and the deep-in-thought look on his face disappears. "Nothing."

I consider asking him to elaborate beyond "nothing" but I'm not sure I want to know what he's thinking. Confessing my role in my stepfather's death was enough for today.

He pulls me into his chest and holds me close. "Don't keep something this big from me again. Not when it's eating you up inside. I'm always on your side, Ashley. I'm not your mother."

"No. You're undefinable."

"Is that a good thing?"

I grip the arm of his flannel. "I'm not sure. You and me... we've always been weird."

"Why are we weird?"

"You tell me." I can't believe we're having this conversation, and I truly can't believe I'm broaching it sober, but out here in the middle of nowhere, I feel okay to be vulnerable. And open.

"Tell you what?"

"Oh, come on, J." I sit up straight and narrow my eyes at him. "We would be there for each other in the absolute shittiest of moments, right? Then, we'd go weeks, months sometimes, barely staying in contact."

"You've always been my best friend, Ash." His voice is raw. "I'm sorry if I didn't make that clear."

"You did!" I hate that I sound so emotional, but after baring my soul to him about my darkest secret, I'm like an open wound. I work to restrain myself. "I don't mind the way we were. The way we are. I love it, actually." I nearly keep talking, but then I stop.

Jared doesn't take his eyes off of mine.

"Why does that feel like an *I love it, but* kind of thing?"

I guess it does. I guess when I'm truly honest with myself, I feel...

"Spit it out, Hill." Jared's tone is teasing, but I can hear the weight behind his words. He's on edge.

"I feel sad, J. I feel like you and I...we both always had so much shit weighing us down from our families that we never had any space to sit with our actual feelings."

His cheeks flush pink. "And what are your actual feelings? Will you tell me now?"

I shake my head. "I haven't worked them out. That's my point. I never thought I deserved to take care of myself and own how I feel. About much of anything. My past still comes to me in my dreams and bites me in the ass. Hell, I had to move across the country to be able to tell you the truth about the night my stepfather was murdered." I look straight at him. "What about you? Have you healed from your past?"

His dark eyes turn nearly black, and I can read him perfectly.

"You want to run like hell right now," I say to him. "I do too. But I'm asking you not to."

He flinches.

"Don't, Jared. Please don't run from this."

CHAPTER FIFTEEN

Jared

I close my eyes for a second before opening them and looking at Ashley. At the one person who won't let me shut down.

"I won't run." I may want to jog very quickly at times, but I won't.

She tilts her head. "Promise?"

"I promise."

She smiles. "Good."

"Let's head back. We'll circle back to this conversation tonight when I get home."

"I'm coming to your game," she says.

I don't want to put pressure on her, so I try to hide how much it means to me that she'll be there. "Cool."

"I'm sitting with Mia."

"Then I'll know where to point when I score my first goal."

We ride back to the ranch and tack down the horses. I make jokes and engage in light banter with Ashley, but my mind is elsewhere. By the way she hurries through the brush down, she knows, but she doesn't call me out on it. I appreciate her patience because I'm too emotional right now. If she pushes me again, I may break.

"Raincheck on the muffins?" I ask her as we stand outside our cabin.

"Of course. I need to get going anyway."

We say goodbye, and she hops into her car.

I wait until she's driven away before I reach for my phone.

Liam answers on the first ring.

"We just finished practice," he says. "I'm headed to pick up Lulu. Can I call you later?" Before I can answer, he says, "Shit. You've got your opener. What time are you leaving for the arena?"

"Not for a while, but this will only take a minute."

"Shoot."

"You know your detective contact at the police station? The one you kept up with before we nailed Dad's killer?"

"Pete. Yeah."

"I need to talk to Pete. Ashley's got this...well, I can't really divulge..."

"No need. I'll have him call you."

"Thanks."

"You and Max kick some ass tonight."

I shake my head as Liam ends the call without asking a single question as to why I need help from the New Orleans police force.

My oldest brother trusts his three younger brothers. Probably more than he should have, at least when we were teenagers. But he'll do anything for us. Including skipping college for himself so he could turn pro and pay for the rest of us to go to school. He had to grow up too soon, but he's the best man I know.

I go home and take care of Louie's food and litter box. She meows as I sit down on the couch and invite her to join me.

I pet her as I go through texts from Max, Coach, and Arch.

All about tonight's game—last-minute ideas and tips regarding our opponent. I answer all the texts and try to relax, but I'm more focused on my conversation with Ashley than anything else.

Something about her story bugs me.

It's the inconsistency of what she said versus who she is.

Ashley never forgot to turn off the space heater before we left her townhouse. Not one fucking time.

So the idea of her suddenly doing something so out of the norm for her—it doesn't add up.

I need to talk to someone who was there the night of the fire. Someone who has access to what was found in the aftermath of the wreckage.

I hate seeing Ashley suffer. It killed me this morning when her eyes filled with so much damn pain. The fact that she blames herself? It slays me.

She's always given me everything of herself. And I don't think I've repaid the favor nearly enough. Maybe I can help her now.

Yes, Ashley has always pushed all my buttons but only in the best way. She's challenged me to keep my heart open. To feel my pain. I've shut down a lot in my life, but she never gave up on me.

And back when I was seventeen, she saved my soul.

It was three months after she had to help her mama bury her stepfather and move into a run-down apartment on the wrong side of New Orleans.

And here I was, standing in her bedroom in the middle of the night with my hands and jeans stained red from dad's blood. She gazed up at me with wide eyes. From her bedside table lamp, I could see the violet flecks in them, and I read the worry in her expression.

I opened my mouth, and all I could say was, "My dad was murdered."

Ashley gasped, but before she could ask any questions, I said in a dark tone, "And if it takes me until I die, I'll find that fucker and make him pay."

Ashley's face had gone pale at my news, but the color came back into her cheeks then. "You'll make sure he's found. And I'll help you."

I just stared at her, my broken heart filled with love for this girl. She had no clue what had happened, but she didn't ask me any questions. Instead, she took my hand and turned for the bathroom.

"But first," she said, "let's get you cleaned up."

An hour later, we were lying in her bed. Neither of us said anything for a few minutes.

"Karma," she said abruptly.

"What do you mean?"

"Karma is on your side. It will help catch the killer and bring justice to your family."

I lay on my back and stared into the dark room.

"Ash."

"Yeah."

"I don't know if I believe anymore."

She was quiet.

"In God."

"I knew what you meant."

"Have you ever lost faith?"

Ashley and I often attended church together. Just the two of us, or sometimes her mom came too. Neither of us was super religious, but church was the one thing Ashley and her mom would do where her stepfather didn't tag along or try to stop them from doing it. It was their safe place.

I liked going to church with Ashley. It felt like something bigger than me, bigger than the screwed-up world I lived in, was present when I sat in the wooden pew with Ashley by my side.

"All the time," Ashley whispered from the pillow next to mine. "Every time my stepdad got violent. But I always tried to put my trust in a higher power. I had to or else...honestly, I couldn't have gone on."

"I feel lost now that my dad is..." I couldn't say the word.

Dead was too final. Too real.

Ashley wrapped her arms around me. She was under the covers, and I was on top of them, but the gesture was so intimate that I fought back tears for the first time since I saw my dad covered in blood at the convenience store.

"Shh." She kissed my cheek. "I'm here."

I took a deep shuddering breath.

And then I told her the whole story.

How my dad couldn't go to our hockey game tonight because he had to work. He always took whatever extra shifts he could get as a desk clerk at the local convenience store. He did it for my brothers and me— so there would be enough money to pay for ice skates and hockey equipment and to have an old, beat-up truck so we could drive to leagues two hours away from home because there was no ice rink in New Orleans.

And then I told her how, on our drive home from the game, we decided to stop in at the convenience store like we often did to say hi to Dad.

We knew something was wrong as soon as we pulled into the parking lot.

The ambulance.

The flashing lights of cop cars.

A deadly silence hit our truck for a split second before Liam jammed the brake, and we all jumped out.

And then a guy dressed all in black pushed past us. I looked right at him. His eyes were dead inside. I knew he was bad news. He disappeared behind the store.

I wanted to chase after him. I had a sick feeling in my stomach, and I turned to go after him.

But Max grabbed my arm. "Dad. We have to check on him."

Liam insisted on going in first, and we all crashed in after him.

A cop was right there in our faces trying to stop us from going further. Once he learned our father worked here, he let us through.

"There's been a shooting," he said in a low tone.

I flinched.

It was a moment I wish I could forget—the moment before.

Before life changes forever. In the worst way imaginable.

If I could rewind that night to before I saw blood on the floor...that would be my one wish in life.

"No!" I screamed as I looked around wildly. Maroon. Red. The colors were melding together, and the multiple puddles led to the cashing counter.

I dashed around it, and there Dad lay on the ground. He must have come out from behind the counter to try to get the killer to leave, and then he went back to the cash register to try to save the money. It's just like Dad...he'd do anything to protect his own.

"Fuck, no. Dad." I kneeled down and reached for his limp hand.

He was alive but unconscious. He moaned lightly, and I hung on to him, not wanting to let him go.

Blood was everywhere, but all I could do was stare at my father's face and beg for him to wake up.

It wasn't to be.

Hours later, he was pronounced dead at the hospital.

And my faith died with him.

"It didn't die." Ashley kept her arms around me. "Your dad will always be with you in spirit. Always."

I didn't believe her. Not even a little. To me, being there meant you were there physically. Having lost my mom when I was young after a long battle with cancer, I leaned on my father to be both parents.

"He's gone," I whispered to her. "I'm officially parentless."

I was nearly an adult, but not quite. And I didn't feel ready to take on the world with no one out ahead of me breaking my falls.

Over the next couple of months, I fell into a state of indifference. I didn't want to die, but I didn't want to be here if Dad wasn't here with me. All I could do was go out every day after school and try to find his killer. Liam and I went together—Hunt was too young, and we all wanted to protect him as best we could, and Max left New Orleans to do a PG year in Minnesota and focus exclusively on hockey.

Not having Max around was hard for me. Harder than I ever let on. Max was my twin, my mirror, the one who'd been with me always, even in the womb. And him leaving right after Dad's death felt like another kind of loss. I would never tell him that, of course, but I damn sure wished I could have gone with him. Liam wanted to send me too, but I'd *never been a good student. Max had the grades to get him accepted into a school out of state, and I didn't.*

Once Max left home, I put all my energy into searching for Dad's killer—and ice hockey. What little time I had left over went to partying with people who wouldn't get too deep on anything.

But Ashley didn't give up easily. She showed up every Sunday morning at my house and dragged me to church with her. I was often hungover and always complaining, but she insisted it would be good for me. The only thing I won on was that we could take my truck. For the first month, I sat next to her numbly, barely listening to the pastor.

Then, one Sunday, on the drive to church, a familiar song came on the radio.

Ashley bounced up and down in the shotgun seat and pointed at the dashboard.

"That's your dad's favorite song!"

I swallowed hard.

"It's a message from him, J," she said softly.

It was hard to argue her. This wasn't some current pop tune; it was an oldie about love and loss and not one I'd heard on the radio in years.

Emotion hit me.

But I held back the tears.

"That was a request by Fran," the radio DJ said as the song ended.

Chills went down my spine.

Fran was my dad's nickname.

"Fran lost his truck in the storm last week, and that's his favorite song," the DJ continued.

Ashley's small hand took hold of my large one and held on.

"Fran. Storm. That's your daddy."

Since we buried Dad, I felt like I'd been carrying around a boulder's worth of guilt that I wasn't there to stop the bastard from killing him. I was numb and walked through my days like I was barely present. Nothing felt like it mattered anymore.

But that day, when we sat together in church, I listened. To the sermon. To Ashley whispering little jokes to me. To the organ music and the people around me and the birds above as we walked out and back to my truck.

"Thank you," I said to her as I dropped her off at her mom's. "I don't know what I'd do without you."

She winked at me as she stepped out. "You'll never have to find out."

CHAPTER SIXTEEN

Ashley

Go, go, go. I sit on the edge of my seat, hands fisted under my knees as I track Jared's progress on the ice. He evades one defender, but when he crosses the blue line, he flips the puck to his teammate, Arch, whose shot hits the goalpost.

Damn.

I relax back into my seat, trying to quell the butterflies.

The first game of the season sets the tone for the rest of the year. It's a big deal. And I want Jared to do well so much it hurts.

"You look hot." Emerson smiles at me as we sit side by side in Declan's box.

"Thanks." I glance down at my black mini skirt and matching leggings paired with a silk turquoise top. My combat boots complete the look. Oh, and I'm wearing make-up. Like actual makeup of mascara, blush, the works.

I never make a lot of effort on my appearance. A swipe of eyeliner and a dab of lip gloss at most, maybe a quick pony, and I'm ready to go. But I spent way too much time getting ready for the game tonight. I even video-called Winter and Peyton for outfit advice, and they correctly reminded me that this isn't like one of those games where Jared's team comes to New Orleans and I haven't seen him in months.

"You live together now," Peyton said before she and Winter burst into laughter.

I laughed along with them, but inside, I was wishing I could feel as lighthearted about the whole *roommates* thing as I sounded.

As the first period winds down with no score by either team, I focus my gaze on number twenty-one for the home team with the surname Storm across the back. Jared skates effortlessly to the bench, and I resist the urge I have to call out to him in support.

He would think it was weird because I never do that, not that he would hear me anyway. I purse my lips and turn to smile at my suitemates. I'm sitting between Haley and Emerson, and Mia and Jamie Beth are on Haley's other side. Mia and Jamie Beth are chatting with Declan and a couple of the other owners to Mia's right.

"It's surreal to be in a box," I admit. "I can still remember driving to Baton Rouge with the girls to watch the Storms play in a run-down rink on the bad side of town."

Emerson laughs. "Times have sure changed since we were all kids."

"Was it hard when Jared moved away for college and then the pros?" Haley asks me.

"I was happy for him," I deflect rather than answer her actual question.

"Would you see him when he came home to Louisiana over the years?" she asks.

"Usually."

That sounds far too casual.

Because the reality is that Jared would call me each time he was coming to town. Winter and Peyton didn't even know. I knew they'd ask well-meaning curious questions, and I had no answers for them. Jared and I were friends. Just friends. As much as that burns to admit. And we were both at fault for the way we ignored any sparks. I was as stubborn as he was, and I dated just as casually if I'm being honest. I may not have had the wide range of dating options that a high-profile athlete did, but I certainly didn't lack for dates.

But whenever Jared was in town, we would meet up after games. Sometimes he would stay the night. If that was the case, maybe we'd hang out for a bit. Then I'd bounce. I didn't want to watch Jared party. And I didn't want to be a part of his world, the world where all the girls throw themselves at him.

But he'd always text me later that night.

I'd be driving home or climbing into bed, or sitting on my couch with a cup of tea.

"You're blushing."

I come out of my memories to find Emerson smiling at me.

"I got lost in the past."

"Seems like a good kind of lost," Haley says.

It was the good kind. The best.

"Ash." He always said my name in a low tone, conspiratorially, like he and I were the only ones who knew what we had.

"J. Great to see you tonight."

"Thanks for coming."

"Did you have fun with all your fans?"

Four beats of awkward silence would follow.

"I don't want to know," I'd say.

"Nothing happened that means anything."

I believed him. I didn't like things to mean too much either. Because that meant the fall could break me.

So I fooled around meaninglessly.

I liked dating guys I knew weren't the real deal. I liked sleeping with them too.

I wanted a real relationship.

That was my end game.

But I couldn't do it. I couldn't commit.

It was too scary.

I told Haley I'm not casual, but the whole truth is...

I can't be casual with Jared.

Anyone else was fair game.

"Can I come pick you up?" he'd say.

"I'll be ready when you are."

In a way, that exchange summarized our relationship.

I needed Jared to pick me up from the valley I lived in, and we were both waiting for the other to be ready.

When, in reality, neither of us was willing to take that risk.

It wasn't safe.

Let another person into his life who could break his heart? He couldn't.

Risk being trapped like my mom? No.

So we stayed separate, jousting like fencers and neither of us surrendering.

But, sweet Lord, those times with me sliding into Jared's truck and driving through the city were some of my happiest moments as an adult. We would talk and catch each other up. Anything I needed help on, he'd offer a suggestion, or he'd just listen. It was different than when we were kids. It was better.

However, when the time came for him to leave town, that was it. A quick hug and a wave with no mention of me visiting him or him coming to see me in the off-season. He often came back to New Orleans when hockey was over, but he didn't stay long. Jared always reminded me of a caged animal when he was home—like he had to get back out into the wild even if it was dangerous.

As the second period begins, my gaze follows Jared as he barrels across the ice. He possesses the puck from the midline until he spots Max up ahead. One quick flick of the wrist and he's led his twin perfectly. Max lets go and slams the puck toward the goal. But...

The goalie makes an incredible save.

And the score remains zero to zero.

By the time we hit intermission, the box is buzzing with frustration.

"God, this is stressful," Emerson says.

It is.

I used to feel right in the middle of the action when I would sit in the stands, but I welcomed any distraction, and I would have loved sitting in a luxury box with snacks and a bar, not to mention all the people in the suite milling around and chatting. But tonight, I'm invested in the game. I'm invested in Jared. I feel a pang of terrified vulnerability at this admission, but I can't deny it.

CHAPTER SEVENTEEN

Jared

"Let's fucking get going!" Arch shouts in the locker room. "We're better than these guys."

He's not just saying that. The San Jose Thunder don't have the roster depth that we do, and our goalie was all-pro the last three years. But the Thunder goalie is playing out of his mind tonight, and we haven't gotten it done.

"We need to play up to our potential," Tex Williams, one of our captains, says, waving an emphatic fist in the air.

"We will," I vow, standing up from the bench and grabbing my helmet. "Let's go, boys."

As we file out of the locker room and back onto the ice, I glance up toward Declan's box.

I saw Ashley before the game started, and I spot her now. She's too far away for me to get a good view, but I can make out her profile.

I promised her I'd score a goal for her.

Time to make good on that promise.

———

Ashley

"Third period's starting." Emerson nudges me. "Maybe somebody will finally score."

The Wild Kings come out with a lot of energy, and the first few minutes are a frenzy of players crashing up against the boards and fighting for control of the puck.

But scoring remains at a premium.

Shots are fired, and both goalies are more on fire than the offenses.

"The Thunder goalie has made some amazing stops tonight," Emerson says.

"He has." I tug at my hair nervously. "The Kings really need this game."

As time winds down, I find myself standing with my arms resting over the bar of the suite. The energy in the arena has gone from excited to frenzied with fans screaming and stomping their feet.

The players seem to pick up on the energy of the crowd.

Arch wins a face-off, and I'm sure this is it.

But then Max gets sent to the penalty box for roughing.

Being down a man, I sit down again, anxiety filling my body.

"They can't score when they're shorthanded," I mutter to Emerson and Haley.

"They can," Emerson says confidently. "Last season, the Wild Kings had the highest percentage of shorthanded goals in the league."

"Really?" I could hug her. "That's a great stat."

"I know. They'll score here. I can feel it."

She's so confident, and I envy her that. She's not just confident in the Kings; she's confident in Max. She knows without a shadow of a doubt how much he loves her, and she, him.

"You and Max are lucky," I murmur, not actually meaning to say it aloud until I hear the words pop out of my mouth.

Thankfully, the sudden roar of the crowd drowns out my words.

Only one minute remains, and Jared and Max are in the middle of a pile of players on the opposite side of the rink from our box.

Jared breaks out of the pile with the puck, and he deftly handles his stick as he races down the ice toward the opposing goal. He sends it over to a streaking Arch, who hesitates just long enough for Jared to break free again.

Arch lets the puck go, and Jared flicks it forward. He's skating so quickly I strain to follow his jersey number. When he releases the puck, I know before it happens that it's a goal.

I start jumping up and down and screaming.

"Goal!" I hear from others in the suite.

The other Wild King players mob Jared on the ice, and the announcer says the Thunder have called timeout.

Still enough time for a miracle.

As the Kings stop celebrating and regroup, Jared turns toward our box and raises his stick.

I flush. That was for me. Just like he said he would do.

I raise my hand and wave before taking my seat again.

Emerson isn't the only one smiling at me when I turn to face my seatmates.

Mia, Jamie Beth, and Haley are all beaming.

"He's totally smitten," Emerson says with a confidence I don't feel. "A Storm brother won't salute just anyone."

"Completely true," Mia agrees as she leans across Jamie Beth's lap enthusiastically. "I think you should go for it if you want to."

Oh, I want to.

And this vote of confidence makes the idea even more tempting.

But I don't know if I can hook up with Jared and walk away. And I would need to be prepared for a one-night stand. Earlier today, I practically confessed I have feelings for him, for God's sake. Feelings that I've never taken the time to process.

And he didn't say anything back.

The fear in his eyes said everything, though.

So I need to make sure I keep my guard up. No matter what happens physically, emotionally, I need to protect myself.

The timeout is over, and the Thunder make one last furious push to score by pulling their goalie and going all in.

It doesn't work.

The Wild Kings pull it out, a tough season opener but one that ends in a victory.

"Yeah!" Declan kisses Mia, and the rest of us hug.

Mia says she's leaving with Declan, and Jamie Beth and Haley follow.

"Come with me to wait for Max?" Emerson asks me. "I hate to wait alone."

Her eyes are mischievous, and she's clearly full of shit, but I want to see Jared too much to turn her down.

I put one foot in front of the other with a feeling in my gut that tonight is going to change everything forever. And I'll have to live with the consequences, good or bad.

CHAPTER EIGHTEEN

Jared

"Let's go out for drinks," Arch says to Tex and me.

I know what that's code for—picking up women—and I'm not interested.

"I'm going home." I grab my jacket out of the locker and shut the door.

"How come?" Tex says, running a towel over his head to dry his red hair. "First game's over. Victory celebration. Let's go!"

"Nope. I'm good."

Max turns around at his locker. "You okay?"

Having all the curious eyes on me pisses me off. What's going on between me and Ashley is personal, and even my twin isn't privy. What she told me earlier today is still raw, and my urge to protect her is stronger than ever.

"I just said I was good," I snap at Max.

Max smirks. "Really? You don't sound so good."

We glare at each other with me silently telling him to fuck off.

Arch raises an eyebrow at me. "What's up with you?"

"Nothing. I'm just not in the mood to go out."

"Raincheck and we'll do dinner instead."

I fist-bump him. "Deal."

All feels smoothed over as he and Tex make their way out of the locker room. The rest of my teammates follow.

I'm relieved they're gone. I want to be alone. But Max hangs back.

"I'm fine," I say immediately.

"You're not. Your focus is somewhere else." He takes a seat next to me on the bench. "You just took over the game tonight. Willed us to win. Coach presented you with the game puck."

That did mean a lot. To start off the season feeling in control on the ice was a big win for me personally as well as the team.

"I've got other things going on besides hockey," I say.

"Like what?"

"Why are you pressing?" I say to him. "It's unlike you."

"True. You usually take that role. But maybe it's time I pushed you a bit."

Here's the thing about living two thousand miles away from your hometown—you don't have to answer to the people who know you best. The ones who know all your tells, the good and the ugly.

I'm luckier than most because my twin brother lives away from home with me. But even Max can't get inside my head all the time. And the truth of it is that my twin and I have been so used to dealing with our own crap privately that we don't always push the other enough when something seems off. Up until he got together with Emerson, my brother was particularly reclusive, and I could pretty much do what I wanted without him getting into my business.

"Emerson has changed you," I say without a trace of malice.

"Good."

I agree. Except for right now.

"Let's just call it a night and go our separate ways," I say. "You can't fix my problems."

"And you couldn't fix mine. But you wanted to."

I did want to. And I hated seeing my brother, the person who's a reflection of myself, suffer.

"Look," Max says, and I can tell he's shifting into a gear that's not comfortable for him. "Is Ashley the girl you were going to ask to Prom?"

I suck in a deep breath before blowing it out. "You never asked me that before."

"I didn't want to pry."

I don't say anything.

"But I wish I had. I'm sorry."

I jerk my head up to look at him. His eyes are filled with pain.

"Don't apologize for something you didn't do wrong." I slap his back. "It's all good, little brother."

He chuckles. "Nice try. *Twin* brother."

I pause. "She was that girl. She *is* that girl."

"But then Dad died."

"Right. And things blew up. So Prom didn't matter anymore."

"It *did* matter. That's the thing, Jared."

"Maybe so." I consider telling him more, but I hold back. "Prom didn't fit Ashley and me anyway."

"What does fit you two? Maybe it's time you figure that out."

Maybe so.

I wave toward the exit. "Go enjoy your evening. Tell Emerson hello."

He pats my shoulder before leaving.

I wait until I'm sure he's gone before I check my phone.

Voicemail.

I play it back.

"Jared, this is Pete Connor from the New Orleans PD. Liam said you have some business you'd like my help with. Give me a call anytime or send me a text. Happy to help if I can."

Realizing it's far too late to call, I shoot him off a text right away.

———

Ashley

We end up chatting with Jamie and Haley in the box while Declan and Mia are busy, so by the time Emerson and I reach the partitioned area by the lockers, the players are already filing out.

Tex and Arch go by first. They say hello and wave. Loads of teammates follow, but no sign of Jared or Max.

"Where the heck are they?" Emerson wonders.

"Maybe they're talking with a coach or still doing an interview," I suggest.

We pass the time chatting about Montana.

"When winter comes, it *really* comes," Emerson says with a laugh. "You won't mistake it."

"I'm not looking forward to the freezing temperatures," I say.

"The positives are hot cocoa and a warm fire and snuggling up with a lover." She smiles fondly.

"I can get behind the first two," I say to her.

We're still chatting when the door swings open and Max comes out alone.

"Where's your brother?" Emerson asks him.

"Still in there." He kisses her gently on the lips. "Ready to go home?"

She glances over at me. "Ashley needs a ride."

"I'm fine," I say hurriedly. "You two go ahead."

Max assesses me. "My brother's in a mood."

"Super," I say breezily. "Well, you know I can handle a Storm."

He tilts his head toward the door he just came through.

"He'll be out in a minute. Maybe he'll share with you what the hell's up with him. I gave it my best shot, but you know Jared."

That I do. He likes to talk but not often about the deep stuff.

Emerson hugs me goodbye with a whisper to call her.

Once they're gone, I take a seat on a nearby plastic chair and pull out my phone.

I'm busy scrolling when I feel a light tap on my head.

Without looking up, I say, "Hey, J."

CHAPTER NINETEEN

"Ash."

"Congrats on the game. How's it feel to be the hero?"

He comes around to the front of my chair and kneels down so we're at eye level.

"I like when you talk me up."

I smile. "I'm sure you do."

From the way Max had talked, I was prepared for Jared to be locked down emotionally, the way I've seen him get when he feels the need to put up his guard.

But his eyes are open and warm. He grins at me conspiratorially.

And I sense a dare coming on.

Jared and I have played the dare game on and off through the years. Often, we did it to help the other get through a tough time. Or a confusing time. Really, anytime we wanted something but were hesitating.

J, I dare you to apply for a hockey scholarship to your reach college. The one Max will get into but you're not sure you can.

Ash, I dare you to interview for the job you may not be qualified for on paper, but you know you could pull it off better than anyone else.

"I dare you to go swimming with me in the pond outside our cabin."

I narrow my eyes. "When?"

"As soon as we get home tonight."

"Why?"

"Because." His eyes flare with heat before he blinks it away. "You love the water. You always have."

True. But that look from him? That wasn't about swimming. That was so hot I could fan myself right now.

It was seriously enough to set me on fire. And more than enough to let me know what's on his mind.

"Tonight?" Goodness, that came out squeaky. "Why tonight?"

His eyes darken, and my stomach flips over. *He's flirting with me. For sure.*

"Because I want to celebrate our first win of the year and you moving to Montana. It's a full moon tonight, and it's unseasonably warm."

It is warm. Hot, in fact. I'm freaking on fire.

"You're on. Let's go home." I stand up with shaky legs and follow him down the hall and out of the arena to his truck.

As I climb into the shotgun seat, the feeling hits me that, after tonight, nothing will be the same again.

CHAPTER TWENTY

Because I was moving to Montana and didn't think swimming would be high on the list of activities, the only swimsuit I packed is a string bikini, which is far skimpier than I'd prefer. Oh, well. C'est la vie. You only live once, right? Having Jared see me in a skimpy bathing suit while living together probably isn't on the list of smartest things I could do tonight. But that's kind of been the theme since I landed in Montana.

———

"It's chillier than I thought it was." I wrap my towel tighter around my waist and pull the hood of my sweatshirt over my head.

Jared throws his arm across my shoulders and hugs me into his side. "I'll warm you up."

New Orleans Ashley would crack a bad joke and slide out from under his muscled arm.

But Montana Ashley clearly has less willpower because I let Jared's arm stay where it is around my shoulders, and I enjoy the closeness.

My body certainly approves. My stomach is in excited knots the entire walk to the pond.

When we reach the dock, Jared immediately pulls his shirt over his head in one smooth motion and, without hesitation, dives into the water.

Crap.

Now I have to join him, or he'll call me chicken. I let my towel drop to the wooden boards of the dock and dip one toe in the water.

"It's cold!" I shout.

Jared's head is bobbing above the water, and in the light of the full moon, I can see him clearly. "It's not bad," he calls back.

"Liar." I laugh and pull my sweatshirt over my head before I jump off the dock.

Shit, I'm getting brain freeze. I swim up to the surface, and when I look up, Jared is right in front of me. He slides an arm around my waist.

"You okay?"

I try to speak, but my chattering teeth won't let me.

Jared chuckles and scoops me into his arms. "Let's go warm up."

Within seconds, we're back on the dock, and he's wrapped me up in my towel.

"Aren't you cold?" I ask him incredulously as he stands before me, soaking wet in just black swim trunks, which leave very little to the imagination.

As wet as they are, the fabric clings to his...impressive package.

I avert my eyes and stay focused on his face.

He shrugs. "I'm used to the cold. Hockey rinks are cold. And I've lived here for a while now."

"That's true. Your blood is probably adjusted. Or something."

"Or something." He steps closer to me.

And then he starts rubbing my back.

My towel is between his hand and my skin, and I know he's just trying to warm me up, but his brown eyes haven't left mine.

My teeth are still chattering, but now it feels more like nerves.

Something has shifted between Jared and me. That wall that we both always put up between us feels very tenuous right now. Maybe it was because I let him in on my last secret between us. Maybe it was because I dared him to open up. I didn't call it a dare when I did it, but I probably should have. And Jared surely recognized it as such.

"You're gorgeous. I needed to tell you that."

"Thank you. Are you..."

"Listening to what you said earlier today? Yes. You were right. We always played it safe, didn't we?"

I can barely breathe. Because Jared is *going* there. He's actually going there.

"We don't have to," I hear myself saying in a voice that doesn't sound like me. I sound impulsive and like I'm throwing caution to the wind. "Play it safe, I mean. We don't have to."

I watch his Adam's apple move as he swallows.

God, is Montana like some sort of alternate universe for us?

I shake my head. I'm not drunk, but I feel like I'm under the influence. Maybe it's lust. Whatever it is, I'm having a hell of a time not putting my hands all over Jared. And if I stand here for two more seconds with him looking at me the way he is, I'm going to lose all control.

It takes everything I have to break the eye contact.

"Let's go inside." I turn away from him and begin hustling toward the cabin.

He catches me before we reach the front door.

"I'll get the door."

He opens it, and I step in ahead of him.

I know I should head for the shower and then go to sleep.

I'm cold, wet, and I feel like I'm having an out-of-body experience. Logical, casual Ashley has been replaced with risk-taker Ashley.

And I'm lost. For the first time in my life, I'm not in New Orleans.

My touchstone.

I reach the couch, and then I turn and look back at Jared.

He's watching me.

He cocks his head like he's trying to read me.

"You okay, Hill?" he says softly.

I shake my head. "I don't know. Maybe I'm homesick."

I expect him to laugh it off. After all, I just left home a few days ago.

But as usual, Jared Storm takes me by surprise.

"It'll get easier. You'll feel at home in Montana in no time."

"I don't have a network here—a team to back me up. I just have myself."

As if on cue, Louie comes up next to me and rubs her sweet furry body against my leg. I squat down to pet her, burying my face in her soft fur.

"Ash."

I look up at Jared, who's stepped closer.

"Yeah?"

"First of all, you've always been enough for you. Right?"

He's right. "Yes."

"And second, you're not alone. You've got me."

I don't remember either of us moving, but all of a sudden, I'm standing up, and we're directly opposite one another.

I reach out and touch his bare chest that's wet from lake water.

He trembles.

I didn't mean to unleash years of pent-up raw lust with that innocent touch, but...

My hand, unbidden, begins to move over the muscular planes of Jared's chest and abdomen.

He sucks in a breath. I'm not looking at his face, but I hear his inhale, and I feel his chest move against the palm of my hand. My finger starts to trace out a word, and then another, on his burning hot skin.

Will he be able to decipher my message?

CHAPTER TWENTY-ONE

Jared

I want you.

Ashley's index finger spells out the three words I've both longed to hear from her and the three words I've prayed she'd never say because I knew I'd be too weak to turn her down.

I *should* turn her down.

But I know I won't.

"I want you too."

At my admission, she jerks her head up.

Her cheeks are flushed red, and I can read her like my favorite book. She's red with lust and a touch of embarrassment.

I step into her and lower my head to whisper into her ear. "Let's go shower."

She takes my hand in hers and leads me into the bathroom.

———

I turn on the shower and adjust the temperature for a minute before glancing over my shoulder.

Holy Christ.

Ashley Hill is naked.

Her bikini lies in a heap at her feet.

And fuck if she doesn't look a million times more beautiful in real life than she did in my fantasies, which is saying a lot. Because I got off a lot on my Ashley Hill castle in the sky.

From her full breasts to those hips I want to grab onto while she rides me, I have to jerk my gaze up to keep my focus on her face.

Her gorgeous eyes pin me in place, and I fight to stay calm and not jump her like a sixteen-year-old.

"Why do I have the feeling tonight's dare isn't finished?" I ask her, my voice coming out rough.

"Here's my dare—you're overdressed, Storm," she says simply.

That can easily be remedied.

I drop my bathing trunks and kick them off my feet. I'm hard and desperate as I step closer to Ashley.

I scoop her into my arms, and she hooks her feet around my thighs.

I kiss her cheek.

Then her nose.

I'm afraid to kiss her mouth because I know exactly how I'll feel—wrecked for anyone else ever again.

Before I can hesitate longer, she shifts, and her lips catch mine.

And holy....

God.

Ashley Hill's mouth is obscene.

Our kiss is...

Beautiful.

A touch sweet.

A lot dirty.

A little poignant for all the years we missed doing this together.

I nibble at her plump lower lip before tugging it gently. She parts her lips, and I slide my tongue inside her hot, wet mouth.

When she moans, I turn and carry her into the shower. The warm water hits my back as I lean Ashley against the tiled wall and hold her close to me. My lips haven't left hers, and her tongue is darting in and out of my mouth.

I let her down slowly until her bare feet touch the tub floor. She breaks the kiss to ask, "Do you have condoms?"

I nod. "In my suitcase."

She slides her hand between my legs. Her fingers encircle my erection, and I groan.

"Darling, keep touching me."

Ashley never stops stroking my dick, which is hard as nails. I gently take her wrist to stop her motion.

"My turn," I say before dropping to my knees before her.

I don't delay. I put my mouth between her legs and grip her thighs as her legs shake, and she tugs on my hair.

"Jared. Oh shoot, that feels good."

Ashley tastes so fucking good. I lick and kiss her as she opens to me. When she goes over the edge, I stand up and take her into my arms.

"Where are we going?"

"To the bedroom."

———

I pull back the bedcovers before laying Ashley on the bed and climbing in next to her.

"Come inside me," Ashley begs as I roll the condom on and brace myself over her in the bed.

I look at her closely. She's as turned on as I am, but an emotion flashes in her eyes.

"Are you okay?" I say quietly.

She widens her eyes. "Why would you ask me that? Of course I'm okay. More than okay, in fact. You just gave me an amazing orgasm not five minutes ago."

"I remember." I kiss her hard before pulling back so I can

lock eyes with her again. "But that was five minutes ago. Like you said, this is now." I draw a line from her lips to between her breasts, and she shivers.

Going on instinct, I flip us so she's on top of me.

Ashley visibly relaxes.

"Are you sure?" she whispers.

"Darling, any position with you is perfect." I grip her hips and angle her over me.

And she takes me inside her.

One thrust and I'm dying from how damn good it feels.

"Fuck, Ash." I halt my movement. "You're so..."

"So what?" She stops too. "Why'd you pause?"

Because I know I'll never be able to forget this. And I don't know what tonight means for us.

"I want to do this again," I hear myself saying. "Promise me."

She brings her face to mine and kisses me. "I promise. Now, will you please fuck me?"

"Gladly." And I do.

CHAPTER TWENTY-TWO

Ashley

The bright light shining on my face wakes me. Thank God it's the weekend and I don't have to work.

I open one eye and see the sunlight streaming through the window.

I can feel the warm little body of Louie at my feet.

And I can definitely feel the heavy arm of Jared Storm wrapped around my middle.

I can't believe I slept with him.

My back is to him, and I keep still, wanting to put off the inevitable a little longer—that moment when Jared and I make eye contact and have to acknowledge that our friendship is forever changed.

"Morning, Ash."

I stop trying to breathe quietly. "How'd you know I was awake?"

"I could tell." He drags his hand down to my bare thigh. "Should we get it over with?"

"What?"

"The face-to-face awkwardness."

"I'm not sure."

"Come on. Let's do it." His voice is tinged with humor.

I turn in his arms until I'm staring into chocolate brown eyes with flecks of green.

"See?" His eyes crinkle at the corners. "Not so bad, right?"

Wrong. This feels so out of my league of manageability.

Jared takes over the bedroom. Any room. But in my bedroom —or I guess, technically, our bedroom—he's all I see.

"It's bad, J." I sit up, realizing too late that I'm naked and Jared can now see my breasts fully.

He saw it all last night anyway.

What I care about is losing my best friend.

"This will fuck everything up," I whisper to him.

"It won't." He sits up and cups my cheeks with his hands. "You and I will be good, Ashley. I know it."

"How do you know that?"

"The same way I know that your favorite color is purple." He lifts his hand off my cheek so he can point at my purple suitcase in the corner of the room. "Just like I bet I can guess what t-shirt you brought with you to Montana for sleeping in. Does it have a duck on it with a cute little phrase?"

I stare at him. "You're so damn cocky."

He raises his eyebrows. "Shall I go prove it?"

I cross my arms over my bare breasts. "No. My Duck Off So I Can Relax t-shirt is with me."

Jared chuckles. "I'm glad. I love that shirt on you."

"You do?"

"Yep. I love the saying, and I love the way your breasts fill it out."

I push his arm. "That's because I've had it since high school! It's shrunk after being washed and dried a million times."

"I know. And every year, I love it on you more."

"You are such a guy."

"Maybe so, but you know what I recently realized?"

"What?"

His eyes convey an emotion I can't read before he says, "I

don't know anyone else's favorite color or what t-shirt they wear to bed."

I swallow. "What about Max?"

Jared grins. "I'm talking about women, Ash."

"I know. I'm just joking."

"To avoid taking me seriously?"

"Maybe." I blink. "Look, I know last night we promised some things..."

"We promised one thing. That we'd have sex again. With each other," he adds when he sees the teasing look on my face.

God, he's so incredibly attractive. I've been trying not to ogle his ridiculously ripped torso since I woke up, but a woman can only resist for so long.

I want him. He wants me. And last night was the best sex I've ever had, hands down. Jared knows what he's doing in the bedroom, and yes, I'd like more of that. I don't know how long we're going to be able to play with fire like this before one of us gets burned—probably me—but this morning, I want him too much to stop.

I drop my arms, exposing my body.

Jared's gaze drops to my breasts. "Are you..."

"Inviting you to touch me? Yes." I lie back down in bed and beckon to him.

"I don't need to be asked twice."

He pulls the covers over our heads and immediately puts his mouth over my right nipple.

"Oh, God. Jared."

His tongue is turning me on so much I feel like I might come.

"Ash..." he mutters into my breast. "I need to hear you call my name. What do you want?"

"Everything." I don't recognize this girl. I'm literally writhing on the mattress, and while I'm comfortable in the bedroom, I never thought I'd feel at ease with Jared.

I've always liked to be in control with guys. So I've been

choosy about who I sleep with. Who I kiss, who I fool around with too. They were good guys, for the most part, but they were guys I could always be on top with. Literally and figuratively.

I didn't say anything last night when Jared maneuvered us into that position, but I wonder if he sensed what I needed without my saying so.

He always knows what I need outside the bedroom, so I shouldn't be surprised we're so in tune in bed also.

Which is why I squeal when Jared flips me onto my stomach and gently pulls my legs wide apart.

"Wait." I turn my head to meet his steady gaze. "What are you doing?"

"I was going to kiss your clit."

Ohh. Well, that sounds...amazing. And scary. But far too amazing to turn down.

"I want that," I say.

"You sure?"

"Yes. Please kiss me."

"On it," he says before he does just that.

"Ohh, yes. Please keep doing that..." I babble as I clutch the sheets tightly with both fists on either side of my head.

When I feel his finger enter me, I'm done for. An orgasm rips through me, and I'm still trembling when Jared grips my hips and pulls me up onto my knees.

"Can I..."

"Yes," I say. That is the only word I ever want to say to Jared in bed.

Out of bed, we spar and argue, and I love saying no to him. But in the bedroom, I want him in every way possible. And I'm starting to love how he takes charge.

"Are you sure you're okay with this? I don't want to do anything you're uncomfortable with."

"Yes, yes, yes." My legs are trembling, and I'm so turned on I barely remember my own name. "Jared, please."

"I love hearing you say that, Hill." His hard cock slides into me from behind, going so deep I bow further into the bed. My cheek presses against the mattress, and Jared's mouth comes down onto mine as he drives into me further.

"You're a fucking goddess," he mumbles against my lips. "So fucking gorgeous. You're so damn wet. I'm going to come so hard."

Oh, God. I'm drowning in lust. Absolutely fucking drowning right now.

Jared drives in and out of me slowly but with an intensity I've never felt before. And I'm climbing again. *Shit.* Could I actually be about to...

CHAPTER TWENTY-THREE

I let out a surprised moan as I come for the second time this morning.

And this orgasm is not a small follow-up. This climax has wings, and I ride the crescendo as I feel Jared follow me with his own. He groans and clutches my hips as he buries his face in my sweaty neck.

"The. Best. Ever."

I'm shaking and limp as he rolls onto his side next to me. I curl into him and rest my head on his chest.

Did he just say...

"Yes." His voice is low but clear. "I did."

Crap. I said that out loud, didn't I?

"You did." His tone is filled with amusement.

"I said that too?" I raise my head to look at him.

"You did."

Several beats of silence follow.

"It was the best for me too," I say finally. "You know your way around a woman's body."

He cocks his head like he knows what I'm thinking. "I know my way around *your* body," he says. "I don't want you thinking it's always like this." He kisses my neck. "It's *never* like this, and that's the God's honest truth."

I rub his facial scruff affectionately.

Louie meows.

We ignore her.

She meows again. Louder this time.

When she strolls up to our heads and meows right in our ears, we both laugh.

"I'll go take care of her little box and get her fresh food." Jared kisses my cheek. "Don't move."

Oh, I won't.

Jared isn't gone long, but it's long enough for my mind to start whirling with doubts.

I'm sitting up with the sheet tucked around my breasts when he slips back into bed and sits next to me.

He kisses my forehead, and I put my hand over his.

But then, silence sets in. And I feel the sudden need to fill the space.

So, I turn to face him and impulsively ask, "Do you want to set some rules?"

He furrows his brow like he's genuinely confused.

"Rules?"

"Yes. I've never done this before, so I'm just making it up as I go."

"You've never had sex before?"

I swat at his hand, and he laughs.

"I've never been in a friends-with-benefits kind of situation."

Jared stills for a fraction of a second. If I wasn't watching him so closely, I would have missed the pause.

But then, instead of answering me, he just nods noncommittally.

And I deflate a little inside.

I broached it as friends-with-benefits because I'm not sure what else to call what we did over the last twenty-four hours, but part of me was hoping Jared would label what we're doing as—if not a relationship because I know he doesn't do those—something *real*. Having sex with him sure feels more meaningful than a mere benefit.

But his neutral expression gives nothing away, so I storm ahead—no pun intended. "Okay, so here's what I think we should do."

His eyes haven't left mine.

"We keep having sex as long as we're sharing this cabin," I stammer out. "Which is supposed to be around a month, but if it's less than, we stop at that point. And if it's longer, we keep going. Until one of us gets our own place."

Yes, I'm aware that I sound like I'm thirteen but I can't stop talking. Now that I've word-vomited this much of my ridiculous proposal, I have to see it through.

"So we break up once we stop sharing the cabin?"

"Yes. No strings."

"With an expiration date," he says in a tone I can't read.

"Right." I catch my breath. "What do you think?"

———

Jared

Expiration date.

I want to throw up at the idea of losing Ashley in a month or whenever our shared living arrangement ends. And the fact that she views what we're doing as friends with benefits stings.

But I have no idea how to label what we are either. And the reality is that I'm not cut out for anything serious. I want to be, but I have yet to prove to myself that I can pull it off. I've never tried for more than casual, and from what I know about Ash's dating history, neither has she.

So, while her suggestion is painful, I have to agree with her. For two scarred people like us, not adding pressure to an already-tenuous situation makes sense.

I will never think of Ashley Hill as a benefit. She's a queen. A goddess. And my best friend who I'm interested in exploring more with. One look at her face and I can see the nervousness. It mirrors my own fears about what we waded into last night when we went swimming in the pond.

So, I decide to give her exactly what she's seeking. And I pray we'll be on the same page at the end.

Ashley

Jared's brown eyes assess me for what feels like forever, but he doesn't say anything.

"J." I touch his arm. "What do you think?"

Please say yes so we can keep doing whatever it is that we're doing.

Jared cups my chin so gently I nearly break and ask him for more than casual.

But before I can say anything, he gives his answer.

"Yes."

His phone buzzes immediately. He reaches over to grab it.

When he glances at the screen, his whole demeanor shifts.

"I have to go." He kisses me almost as an afterthought and jumps out of bed.

He grabs his clothes and hurries out of the room and into the bathroom.

I'm lying there, trying to figure out if it was a woman who texted him, when he returns to the bedroom fully dressed.

"That was fast." I don't know what else to say.

Jared's ability to dress to impress without spending a second rivals my own speed. My girlfriends always tease me for my lack of effort put into getting ready, and Jared is similar.

"What happened to that thing you do with your hair?" I gesture to his dark head of hair, which is normally messily styled on purpose but right now is just barely combed.

It still looks gorgeous, of course, thick and short to his head with a touch of length.

"Don't have time today for vanity." He smirks as he leans over to plant a firm kiss on my lips. "See you later, darling."

"See you."

I watch him go before I reach for my own phone.

Emerson texted, asking if I want to meet for breakfast.

I text her back 'yes.'

————

"So you and Jared are dating." Haley raises her hand for a high five as I sit across from her and Emerson at the small-town diner. We've ordered breakfast and are partway through eating already. The two of them have been peppering me with questions since I arrived.

I avoided saying much for a while, but eventually, I caved.

"We're casual," I say quickly. "This is a cute place."

I'm not just deflecting. The Rodeo Diner has a great vibe. Cowboy hats and photos of rodeo events line the walls. The servers wear simple red and blue striped shirts with a picture of a steer on their left sleeve. Haley tells me she comes here every Saturday morning.

"Will you make it social media official?" Haley teases me.

"No!" When I don't meet her high-five offer, she slowly lowers her hand back to her cup of coffee. "I don't think you heard me correctly. Jared and I are engaged in a casual and mutually beneficial sexual arrangement. That's all."

Emerson and Haley are both smiling widely.

"What?" I stab at my hash browns with my fork and eat a mouthful.

"So you're saying that he doesn't want serious?" Haley asks me.

Yes, that's exactly what I'm saying.

"Did you ask him?" Emerson asks me.

"No, I didn't ask him exactly."

More like I told him what we should do. And he readily agreed.

"Maybe you should be blunter," Haley suggests. "Guys can be so bad at expressing themselves. We have to show them the way."

Emerson's watching me. "Did something else happen?"

I exhale. "It's not a big deal."

"Share with us," Haley says.

"Okay, but I'm trying to take everything in stride. The thing is, Jared got a text when we were in bed together, and then he ran out. I know he wouldn't be with anyone else while we're together, but he certainly seemed intrigued by whoever texted him."

"Business call," Haley says confidently. "Hockey related."

Doubtful, but I don't argue her.

Jared *is* guarded, but I'm just as bad really.

"It's just better this way." I point at my breakfast plate. "Wow, these eggs are delicious."

"You're deflecting," Haley says. "I deflect with the best of them. But in your case, I really don't think you need to."

"That's right," Emerson says. "Enjoy your time with Jared. See where it leads."

"For sure," Haley says. "He's hot, you're hot. What's not to like?"

I laugh.

They're right.

I'm going to enjoy the hell out of these next four weeks. When they're over, I'll allow myself to cry, but not until then.

CHAPTER TWENTY-FOUR

Jared

Call me by 11 New Orleans time

I hated to leave Ashley in bed, but Pete's text can't wait. I can't tell her anything until I get some actual information. And I'm not sure that's even possible yet.

As soon as I'm in my truck, I give him a call.

He picks up on the first ring.

"Thanks for taking the time," I begin.

"No problem. Liam said your girl may need some help?"

Your girl.

"Um, she's an old friend who I care about. Her family's home was destroyed by a fire years ago. I'd like more information on the cause, which was said to be the space heater, and the location of where the fire started."

"You may need to talk to the fire chief. But let's see what I can find out on my own. I'll pull up the records from the case and see how much information was given."

"That would be great."

He asks me for Ashley's name and physical address at the time. I give him her stepfather's and mom's names and the month and year of the fire.

He says he'll be in touch as soon as he knows more. I thank him again, and we end the call.

I'm already driving, and practice starts in an hour, so I decide to get there early.

When I arrive at the arena, Max is getting out of his truck. He waves me over, and as I walk toward him, I see he's on the phone.

"Here." He hands me his cell. "Liam."

I take the call. "Hey."

"So the Wild Kings are on our schedule next month."

I chuckle. "I'm aware."

"I thought we could have an impromptu bachelor party for Hunt after the game. I've already asked the team's permission for us to stay the night. We don't have another game until Monday, and it's at home."

"Sounds good." I go to hand the phone back to Max, but Liam's still talking. "And maybe after a few drinks, you'll fill us in on what's up with you and Ashley Hill."

"I don't think..." I start to say.

But Liam's laughing. "I'm messing with you."

"Bullshit," I say. "You're the nosiest of the four of us."

"True. That's part of the calling of being the oldest. We get to pry into our little brothers' business so we can make sure y'all are okay."

My irritation wanes. Liam doesn't just have a young daughter. He's been guardian of the three of us for years, whether it was formal or not. We leaned on Liam for a lot once Dad died, and our big brother never once let us down.

"See you soon," I tell him. "Give Lulu a kiss for me."

As Max and I walk into practice together, he says, "You look less aggravated today."

I know where he's going. "Shut up."

He smiles. "Good night?"

The best.

"So. Are you and Ash..."

"We're not anything anyone would understand."

"Got it."

We lapse into silence as we cross through the lobby and head for the lockers.

"Do you both want to meet Emerson and me for dinner tonight?"

I appreciate his offer.

But I don't think Ashley and I are ready to go public.

"Maybe another time," I tell him as we enter the locker room.

"Just let me know."

"I will."

All I want to do with Ashley tonight is order takeout and hang out.

And maybe get naked with her.

Definitely get naked with her.

———

And that's exactly what we do.

That evening, we go pick up takeout from a Mexican restaurant on Main Street.

We bring the food home and sit on the couch to eat. Louie happily joins us by inserting her furry little body in between us. Ashley picks Louie up and sits her on her lap and then puts her legs over mine as she bites into a tortilla chip dipped in guacamole.

"I never ate much Mexican food growing up," she says. "Pretty sure I missed out."

"You said earlier you love Mexican food."

"I do. I've eaten it a lot since I became an adult. But as a kid, I was pretty boring. I stuck to plain food."

"You were never boring." I run my hand down her leg. "You're the only girl who didn't bore me in high school."

"Really?" She smiles at me teasingly. "So you dated girls who bored you?"

"Yep. I couldn't handle a challenge."

"Me neither." She raises her eyebrows at me. "You're my biggest challenge yet, Storm."

"Oh, yeah?" I lean in to kiss her. "So you're not bored yet?"

"Definitely..." She nips my bottom lip. "Not..." She drags her tongue down my throat, eliciting a groan from me. "Bored."

Louie, recognizing when it's time to go, jumps off Ashley's lap and heads for the bedroom with her tail in the air.

Ashley giggles, but a cute cat can't distract me.

My self-control is so frayed that I can barely keep from skipping all the bases and heading straight for home.

But I want to learn every inch of Ashley's body. So I'm going to take my time.

I slide her sweater up over her ribs until I can kiss her bare stomach.

She squirms when I reach the waistband of her pants.

I unbutton the clasp and lower the zipper slowly.

So slowly my hand is shaking.

So slowly Ashley's breaths become little gasps as she grips my hair with her hands.

"J. Faster."

"Can't." My voice is guttural. "I want to remember every second of undressing you. Last night was so..."

"Hot?"

"Yes. But we rushed."

"We'd waited for so long."

"We had, but tonight?" I drag her pants and underwear down her legs and off until they make a pile on the floor by the couch. "Tonight, we're going to take our sweet damn time, darling."

As I bury my head between her legs, Ashley throws her head back against the couch cushions and moans out my name.

I taste her over and over again. This location is quickly becoming my favorite place in the world.

I'm not there nearly long enough before I feel her climax against my tongue.

I climb up her body and kiss her neck.

But she sits up and flips over so her head is at my waist.

"My turn," she says, echoing my phrase from last night.

I put my hands behind my head and watch as she unzips my jeans and pulls them down until my erection springs free.

I've had my share of oral sex. Given and received.

But when Ashley's full lips close around my hard length, I buck so much I nearly fall off the couch.

As she keeps sucking me off, I go into a state of pure bliss.

I lose focus on everything but the way she's making me feel.

"So good, Ash," I mutter. "So, so good."

I'm watching her up until the moment I come, and then the feeling of ecstasy fully takes over my body and mind. I slam my eyes shut, and I call out her name, not stopping until I finally start to come down from my high.

"Holy shit."

She laughs as she snuggles up next to me and rests her head on my shoulder. "Good?"

I'm breathing heavily, and I can't answer her for a moment.

When I do, I simply say, "Definitely good."

CHAPTER TWENTY-FIVE

Ashley

I wait until we've showered together, engaged in a strenuous round of sex, and climbed into bed before I say what's been on my mind since this morning.

"J."

"Ash." His tone has a hint of amusement in it. "What's on your mind?"

"This morning."

"Yeah? What about it?"

"The way you left."

"Ah."

"Ah?" I sit up in the bed and give him a stern look. "What's that mean? Ah—sounds like you're at the doctor and they're checking your throat for strep."

Now he outrightly laughs. "I've definitely missed your flair for the dramatic, Hill."

"I'm not being dramatic," I say in an overly calm tone.

I'm totally being dramatic.

But I don't want to tell Jared that. I need him to reassure me. Or just be honest with me. That would be more than enough.

Anything else, I can handle. What I can't handle is evasion and, worse—lies.

Jared sits up to face me. I refuse to look at his rock-hard abs and sexy-as-sin pecs, and I keep my eyes trained on his.

He takes my face in both his hands and says gently, "The phone call. That's what has you worried?"

"Of course it's the phone call!" I throw up my hands and shift back from his hands. "It's none of my damn business, though, and that's what bugs me the most."

"Do you trust me?" His expression is neutral, but I can tell how much my answer means to him by the way his voice lifts at the last word.

"Yes. Of course." I lean forward to kiss him. "I trust you."

"Okay." He pulls me into his lap. "I'm glad. Because you can trust me, Ash. I promise."

I'm counting on that. Each time I fall into bed with Jared, I give up a little bit more of my self-protective armor. Which means, with every day we continue to carry on this affair, I'm growing more and more vulnerable.

After he falls asleep, I slip out into the living room and post on social media.

Posting on social media has been my job for a while, and even though I've changed companies, I haven't lost sight of how important it is to build a following.

Mia's company has an extremely loyal group of clients, but she's looking to evolve and grow, especially regarding her foundation. That's where I come in.

I spent the day sitting in on meetings with her and other members of the company, and I feel more inspired than ever to get photos of Wild Ranch and the horses she's brought here to rehabilitate and help heal.

The next morning at the crack of dawn, I help Jared pack for his road trip, and he drives me to the stables before he leaves to meet the Wild Kings.

He parks behind the barn so we can't be seen from the road

or the main house, and we watch the sunrise together. The bright orange is heavenly to view as it comes up over the horizon.

"I don't think I've ever seen something more beautiful," I murmur.

"Me neither."

I glance over.

He's staring at *me*.

Yes, it's cheesy as hell.

But does it feel good to be worshipped for a moment?

Absolutely.

I smile at him. "You're a charmer."

"I'm just honest." He reaches over and brushes the stray hairs off my face. "This has always been my favorite strand of your hair. She's got a mind of her own. She can't be tamed. Just like you."

"That means I've got a wild streak in me. I don't like being owned. Being trapped scares me." I'm testing him. I need to know how he responds because I lay awake last night for quite a while, trying to quell my fears that I'm already in too deep with him. This is why I've never dated by following my heart before. It's scary as fuck.

"I know you're a bird that can't be caged. I know every little nuance of Ashley Hill. All of her turns me on like no one else." Jared clears his throat and puts both hands on the steering wheel. "We both need to go. We shouldn't..."

"Get all riled up?" I laugh. "No. Probably not."

Although my panties are already wet from his words.

I take a breath and work to calm down. I need to go work in a minute, and I don't want to be in a state of arousal when I enter the barn.

We sit quietly in Jared's truck like we don't know how to say goodbye. I loathe the fact that my chest is already tight like I'm losing my best friend when he's only going away for a week.

"This is silly," I finally say. "You'll be back before we can blink."

"Pretty sure I'll blink a few times. My eyes would dry out if I didn't," he jokes.

I playfully slap his arm. "Ha-ha."

"So." His voice is hesitant. "I'll call you every day while I'm away. Before games. After games."

"Okay." I wrinkle my nose at him. "I'm not worried, Storm. About fan girls and all that."

"Good, because you have no reason to worry at all."

He runs a hand through his dark hair, which just makes me want to do the same. I glance around, and, not seeing anyone, I slip onto his lap.

"Your hair's a sexual elixir," I say as I slide my fingers through his thick locks.

He groans. "Shouldn't we talk for a minute and then say goodbye? I don't want to make you late for work."

"It's okay. I'm alone at the ranch right now..." I squeeze my legs around his waist. "And for a few minutes, I want to focus on things that don't involve talking."

"What about dirty talk?" Jared murmurs into my ear.

I kiss his neck. "Dirty talk is accepted. And invited."

"Good." He circles his hands around my ass. "Then I'd like to tell you that I want to feel you ride my cock in this truck."

"Is that a challenge?" I'm already unsnapping my jeans.

"It's a request." He unbuttons his own jeans and helps me to slide mine down my legs.

Within a minute, he's grabbed a condom out of his glove compartment and I'm sinking down onto him with my hands braced on his shoulders for balance.

Jared

Our unplanned lovemaking session quickly turns frenzied.

Ashley's pistoning her hips so fast, and I feel out of control.

With lust.

With desire.

With love.

Wait.

What?

Love.

How the hell did that word get in there?

I push everything out of my mind and hold tightly to Ashley's hips while she urges us both toward a quick but intense climax.

And as I'm coming down from the high, *I love this* is on the tip of my tongue.

There's that word again.

Ashley's staring at me.

"What?" I say softly.

I know her too well to miss the look in her eyes.

Curiosity.

And my girl loves to uncover a mystery.

But now's not the time for confessions. I'm heading off on a business trip, and she's getting comfortable with her new job. Whatever I want to say can wait.

———

Ashley

The heat in Jared's eyes as he looks at me is undeniable, but it feels like more than that. His cheeks flush pink, and his expression is so unguarded it makes me breathless.

I nearly burst into awkward chatter to cover up the intensity. But I can't do that with Jared. So instead, I just stare at him like maybe he'll say something. Anything.

"What?" is his way of breaking the silence.

"Nothing." I kiss him quickly and climb off of him. "I should get going."

I'm still catching my breath as Jared helps me find my underwear.

"How the heck did I manage to lose half of my clothes?" I look underneath the seats to no avail.

Jared holds up my pants and panties from the backseat.

"They escaped to the back," he jokes.

"You're an angel." I take them from him and hurriedly dress.

No one is around, but the faster I get out of a compromised position, the better. For all I know, one of the Wild brothers could come sauntering around the corner any minute.

And the truth is that I'm reeling.

A quickie in a pick-up truck is not unfamiliar territory to me.

I'm from the South. And I've always enjoyed sex.

But the way I felt when Jared was inside me? That's a one-of-a-kind feeling. Overwhelming. Intoxicating. This moment of being with him feels so, so good, but I need a moment alone to process.

"I'll miss you, Ash." Jared hesitates, and for a minute, I'm certain he's going to say more.

Instead, he leans forward and gives me the kiss of my life.

Tongue and tenderness with the perfect combo of urgent and casual. Just like him.

I practically jump out of the truck.

Yep. I'm officially in over my head.

And the scariest part is...

I wouldn't change a thing.

CHAPTER TWENTY-SIX

Jared

I'm still grinning after kissing Ashley when she hops out of the truck and waves goodbye as she walks backward toward the barn.

She keeps walking backward, blowing me kisses the whole way until she nearly bumps into the barn door.

Then she turns and hustles through the door and out of sight.

However, because I know her sense of fun, I wait, and sure enough, not twenty seconds later, she reappears at the nearby barn window to wave one last time.

I wave back, and when she's finally turned away, I put the truck into reverse and back onto the ranch road. I realize halfway down the road that I left my wallet back at the cabin, so I turn back.

As I'm pulling up to the cabin, the memory returns.

Love.

I felt love.

Of course, on some level, I've always loved Ashley.

Adored her.

Worshipped her.

Protected her.

But feeling love for her while we're having sex is a whole other kind of thing.

I've never felt that for another woman.

And it should scare the crap out of me.

And yet...a sense of peace and calmness comes over me when I recollect that moment with her.

Ashley's bare hips in my hands.

Her eyes wide but with a touch of innocence that she miraculously never lost, locked on mine.

Her mouth parted in bliss.

And all I want to do is make her broken heart whole.

The best way I know how to do that is to help heal her past.

Right on cue, my phone buzzes. I turn off the truck and glance at the screen before swiping.

"Hey, Pete."

"It's not in the report."

"I'm not following."

"The location of where the fire started. The officer on duty that night didn't put it into the official police report."

That makes no sense.

"Isn't that unusual?" I ask him.

"Not necessarily. The implication in the report is that the resident was nearby."

"You mean Aaron, the man who died in the fire?"

"Yes."

"Well, who would have the specifics? Someone must, right?" I'm not going to let this go just because someone didn't take good enough notes.

"The fire chief. He's retired now."

I clench my jaw. "Let's reach out to him. Is he in New Orleans still?"

"He is, and I'm already on it. I'm going to see about getting my hands on his report."

"Great. I appreciate it."

"This girl must mean a lot to you, huh?"

"She means the world," I say simply. "And you uncovering this information could change her life."

"I'll do my best. Be in touch," and he clicks off.

I toss my phone onto the passenger seat in frustration.

If the chief has a comprehensive report from that night, it should have the location of the heater listed.

It has to.

If not, I'll find out another way.

I get out of my truck and stare out at the mountains. Maybe I'm wasting my time.

The thought has crossed my mind—in my effort to help ease Ashley's guilt, I'll simply gather proof that the space heater was in her bedroom after all.

But my instincts tell me otherwise.

So I have to trust myself and keep pushing forward.

CHAPTER TWENTY-SEVEN

Ashley

"The foundation's social engagements have shot up in the last week." Mia beams at me. "You have a knack for this kind of thing."

"I'm pretty sure Haley is the one who's driving the engagement." I smile teasingly at Haley sitting next to me.

Mia, Haley, and I are meeting in Mia's office at the end of a long work day as we bounce ideas back and forth and go over the pros and cons of how things are going for Haley and me and a new project, which was a fun idea the two of us came up with last week when she was over at my cabin and we'd finished a bottle of wine together.

We were out looking at the stars in the enormous Montana sky, and I pulled out my phone and started a live social video.

Wild West Ash wishes on a star...with plenty of wine

It went viral, thanks to Haley's ability to ad-lib and be completely herself.

"Should I lick a star?" she said after I introduced her to my followers.

Ever since, we've done a Montana adventure nearly every day after work, and we record each of them live.

We've done a video of us riding two of the rescue horses Mia had brought in via her foundation.

We recorded Haley and me welcoming in a new rescue horse before we went for a round of beers at a local bar new to both of us. I'm pretty sure Haley's insistence on me filming her riding a mechanical bull broke the internet.

Haley laughs. "What can I say? You can take the girl out of social, but you can't take social out of the girl. I love doing live feeds. And Ashley's the perfect partner."

"Our videos were supposed to be all about the horses," I say to Mia. "But then we drank wine. And the videos expanded into us exploring Montana. Two fish out of water women. Me from the south and Haley originally from the northeast."

"I love it." Mia shows us the graphic on her laptop. "And the audience loves it. The foundation's page has so many hits, and we're getting seen. Which is so awesome for the horses and all the ones we still have to help."

Haley pats my arm. "This one's a workaholic. She never stops thinking of ideas."

I do love my job. I feel like I'm always on the job in a sense because I'm constantly thinking of ways to market the foundation.

But ever since Jared left for his hockey trip a week ago, I've thrown myself into work more than normal.

I got bored sitting at the cabin by myself.

I've had more free time with him away.

And mainly, I've missed him.

A lot.

"Has Jared watched your social feed when you do a live?" Mia asks me.

"No," I say. "Jared hates social media."

"He follows you," Haley points out.

"Yes, but he almost never looks at his feed."

· · ·

He did DM me last night, though.

I didn't tell Haley about it.

Wild West Ash does cowboy life was yesterday's video when we filmed ourselves helping Luke herd sheep.

I cut off the recording when I nearly fell off my horse and Luke caught me.

Jared obviously got wind of it because he sent me a terse DM—

Be Safe.

And you don't need a cowboy when you have me.

Is someone jealous? I wrote back with a smiley face.

You have no idea how much was his surprise answer.

And then it turned into a *sexy, dirty, not for others' eyes* kind of direct message.

And he and I had some incredible phone sex afterward.

Tonight, Jared is finally coming home.

And all that pent-up sexual frustration is about to be released. We won't need to have phone sex. We can do the in-person thing. And I plan to do it...*a lot.*

But first, Jared has one last road game to play before he comes home.

"Are you two doing a video tonight?" Mia asks.

Haley holds up a hand. "Ash and I are going to watch Jared's game. Maybe we'll do a live of us cheering on the home team."

———

Jared

"Get it, Max!" I bang my stick hard on the ice and start moving past the Arizona defender. "I'm on your left!"

Max takes control of the puck and pivots. He barrels down the ice and, without looking in my direction, sends the puck over.

Perfect placement and I catch it in stride with my stick. With one flick, I let it go.

Score! Right past the goalie's outstretched leg and into the net.

We're halfway through the second period, and we're already up three to nothing on Arizona.

The rest of the game continues in the same vein. Our first shutout of the road trip, and we win, five to nothing. Overall, it's been a successful trip. Only one loss, and we've bonded as a team.

"You looked good out there," Coach says to me as I leave the ice.

"Thanks, Coach."

"Do you have a new routine this season?" he asks me curiously.

"Why do you ask?"

"You're more focused this year than last. You're skating faster and stronger. And your total points are way up."

"I've got a secret weapon," I tell him.

"Oh, yeah? Well, whatever it is, keep doing it. It's working."

Athletes are, by nature, superstitious. If something works, like Coach says, we keep it going until it doesn't work anymore.

But for me, what's been working is that I'm with Ashley. I sleep better. I smile more. I panic less. She's always on my side, and I feel her support even when she's not with me, like this week.

We've talked daily. Just like I promised her.

And I can't wait to get home to see her tonight.

Her new social media videos have made me feel like I'm right there with her some nights. She's funny and authentic and never tries to be somebody else. Her Wild West stories narrated in her southern drawl are hilarious and warm. I'm biased, of course, but she's definitely really good at her job.

When I reach the locker room, before hitting the showers, I check my phone.

This is a new thing for me. In the past, I would wait to look at my phone because I'd be expecting dozens of messages from women wanting to hook up after the game. It overwhelmed me, I realize now, but it's like I didn't know how to pivot away from that mess I'd willingly gotten myself into. It wasn't the women's fault. It was entirely mine. I was afraid of commitment, so I felt safer having multiple women to flirt with and potentially meet up with.

But since Ashley moved to Montana, I've deleted all those women from my contacts. If they texted, I told them I was no longer available. And if they didn't listen, I blocked them.

My phone is so much cleaner now, and looking at it doesn't overwhelm me anymore. It's filled with cute pictures of Louie and Ashley that Ash has sent me since I've been gone. They make me smile.

As I scroll through my phone now, I take a second to check Ashley's socials.

Sure enough, she and Haley are sitting in the cabin, pumping their fists and pointing at the TV screen, which has the Arizona arena front and center.

"We won!" Haley shouts into the camera.

Ashley laughs, her cheeks pink and her eyes bright. I could swear she smiles right at me when she says, "Hurry home to Montana so you can celebrate with your *true* fans."

I shoot her off a quick text. *On my way, darling.*

As a team, we celebrate in the locker room before filing out to get on the flight home.

I'm about to step onto the team plane when Pete calls me.

"Got it," he says as soon as I answer.

I freeze mid-step, and Max and Arch file past me. Max glances back, but I give him the thumbs-up, and he continues on into the plane.

"What's the verdict?" I ask Peter, realizing my voice is actually shaking.

"Your instincts were on point, Storm. I'm texting you a copy of the report now."

I clutch the phone. "So, the space heater..."

"Wasn't in the kid's bedroom. It was out in the living room by the old man's feet. The living room curtains are what caught fire."

Thank Christ.

I release the breath I was holding. "You have no idea how much I appreciate this, Pete."

"Glad to help, especially a good family like yours. I always liked your daddy. Was an absolute crime what happened to him. You boys did okay for yourselves, though."

"Yes, we did."

"Your dad would be proud, son."

I don't cry even though the tears threaten behind my eyelids.

I don't break down even though a part of me wants to. The part of me that's so fucking tired of being stoic and strong and resolute. Sometimes, I just want to give in to the grief I feel on the daily about all the things my parents are missing by not being here. About all the moments I regret not expressing how much I appreciated and loved them when they were still alive.

Halfway up the steps to the team plane, I stand there on the phone with a virtual stranger, and I fight back the tears I never let flow.

Something about Ashley being released from her prison of guilt has got me going.

"I appreciate that." I thank Pete again and end the call.

And then, I look out over the tarmac to the night sky beyond. I pray for the strength to get past my father's death. I never realized until now how much it's been holding me back. I've done it to myself—I refused to grieve, refused to acknowledge my pain, and it's cost me. I've pushed Ashley away.

But I won't do that anymore.

I'm going all in with her, starting tonight.

I climb the rest of the steps and walk to the back of the plane.

"You want to play gin?" Tex asks me as we settle into our seats.

"Sure."

He deals me in, and Arch joins us as we take off.

A few rounds in, Max asks to play.

"So what's going on with your temporary roommate?" Arch asks me with a raised eyebrow.

Max shakes his head at him. "Don't push it, man."

"I'm not pushing anything," Arch says. "Just making conversation."

"Conversation, my ass," Tex says. "You're dying to know if he's dating her."

"Ashley's an old friend," I say. "I've told you that."

"I remember." Arch takes his turn before adding, "Seems like maybe she's more than that now?"

I consider telling him off for being such a nosy fucker, but his blue eyes are open and his tone genuinely curious.

Arch is as scared of getting into a relationship as any guy I've ever known. We've all got our reasons, and I don't know his. What I do know is that he goes through women like he's allergic to seeing them more than once.

And I can relate. So I put down my cards and shift to face him.

"She doesn't bore me," I say. "No matter how much time I spend with her."

He widens his eyes. "Really?"

"Really."

I see the moment he shutters his expression. He blinks, and the emotion that was in his eyes disappears.

"Well, good for you, man." He returns to focusing on the cards in his hand.

I glance over at Max, who shoots me the barest of smiles.

But I don't need to ask him what he's thinking. I can talk to my twin without speaking.

I'm happy for you.

I haven't committed to anything... I try to argue him.

Don't care. I'm still happy for you.

I give him a head nod.

I still don't know what the hell Ashley and I are in terms of an official label, but I know one thing—I can't wait to see her when we get home.

CHAPTER TWENTY-EIGHT

Ashley

"What do you think?" I ask Louie as she stretches out on the bed.

She huffs and turns around three times before settling with her face away from me.

I can't say I blame her for being exasperated.

I've changed my outfit three times.

Ripped jeans? *Too high school.* They went into the dresser.

Maxi dress? *Too summery.* I took it off.

Yoga pants and a t-shirt? *Too casual.* They went back into the closet.

"I've got it," I say to Louie's back. "The final outfit. You'll see."

I change, and even Louie meows her approval.

Button-down cream shirt and jeans. *Perfect.*

Mood? *Sexy casual.*

Okay, maybe not as casual as I should be.

My heart is feeling pretty vulnerable tonight.

With each phone call from Jared this past week, I opened up a little more.

And tonight, I'm finding it hard to stay guarded. I'm not sure I even want to protect my heart anymore.

I hear the truck pull into the gravel drive.

"J's home!" I say to Louie.

I sprint out of the bedroom and fling open the front door.

"Whoa!" Jared says in surprise as I hurl myself into his arms. "Hey. I missed you."

He smells so good, like soap and ice and him.

"Missed you too." He wraps his arms around me and puts his mouth over mine.

Our kiss is sooo tender. At first.

Then it turns urgent. A little desperate.

A lot hot.

Jared is the best kisser.

The best.

"That good, huh?" he mutters against my lips.

Did I say that out loud?

"Yep."

"This is a bad habit of mine."

"Talking out loud by accident?" He slides his mouth across my jawline.

"Yes." I'm no longer sure what I'm even saying yes to.

All I know is that I don't want Jared to stop touching me.

And he doesn't. He lowers me till my feet hit the floor and then he unbuttons my shirt until I'm exposed to him. My jeans come off next.

His hand goes between my legs. "No panties?" he says with a groan.

"No."

His other hand slides around from my back to my bare breasts. "No bra either."

"I wanted to be ready for your arrival."

He drops his head to my shoulder. "You're killing me, Hill."

I smile as he shifts until his mouth closes over my hard nipple.

"I need you closer," he mutters into my skin.

I'm already unsnapping his pants.

He shifts back from me to shrug off his suit jacket before lifting me and backing us up against the wall. I squeeze my legs around his waist and moan when I feel his hardness press against my core.

"Please tell me you have protection nearby..."

"Got it," he murmurs as he reaches into his pants pocket for his wallet.

"Hurry," I beg him.

"Getting...there." He rips the condom wrapper with his teeth, and I help him pull it out and roll it onto his impressive length.

He tilts his head back so he can look directly into my eyes. "You ready?"

"Uh-huh."

He pushes forward, and I widen my legs as he slides all the way home.

"Christ." Jared stills. "Let's slow down."

"Don't you dare slow down," I tell him.

"But I'm so close."

"So am I." I kiss him. "Super...close. Don't hold back."

And he doesn't.

He pulls out and then drives back in. Over and over.

With each thrust, I get closer to the edge until I'm dangling on the brink of ecstasy.

We each cry out at the same time. His name is on my lips and mine on his as he clutches me to him.

"We're not finished." He kisses me hard and then pulls out of me slowly but doesn't put me down on the floor.

"Where are we going?" I ask as he starts walking with me in his arms.

"The bed." He turns the corner into the bedroom and drops down onto the bed.

Louie's still sleeping at the foot, and he gives her a pat and a snuggle.

"Missed you, little one," he says as she purrs.

I grab my phone to take a photo.

"I'm naked," Jared protests as he puts up his hand to block me.

"So? These pictures are just for the three of us."

He chuckles. "The three of us? You think Louie wants a copy of this photo?"

Louie's purrs grow as Jared and I spar. She stands up, arches her back, and leans in for more pets. Jared obliges until he picks her up gently and puts her on the floor.

"We'll hang out more later," he promises her. "Right now, I'm a little busy."

"With what?" I ask him.

"I want to do what we just did all over again...but slow this time."

"How slow?" I stare up into his gorgeous face. His brown eyes are heated and his lips swollen from kissing me.

"So slow that you'll be screaming for me to go faster." He kisses each of my cheeks and then my lips.

He kisses my jaw. And then my neck. By the time he reaches my breasts, he's right. I'm begging him to speed up.

"Not this time," he says. "This time, we're taking our sweet time, darling."

He pulls the sheets up over our heads and travels south.

———

Two more orgasms later, we finally come up for air.

Jared sits up against the headboard as I lean my head against his shoulder.

"How was your flight home?" I ask him.

He chuckles. "It was good. Feels like a million hours ago."

"We've been a little busy, so I forgot to ask you."

"Speaking of forgetting..." He reaches across me to retrieve his cell phone out of his pants pocket.

"Yeah?"

The seriousness of his tone has me sitting up straight and looking at him with concern. "Everything okay?"

"Everything's fine." He scrolls through his phone before looking up at me. "Ash, I have something to show you."

"Okay." *Why is my stomach in knots all of a sudden?*

"I had planned to show you right when I got home, but then you jumped into my arms, and I forgot everything but getting you naked as fast as possible."

He hands me his phone.

I read the file on the screen three times before raising my head.

His brown eyes assess me, and I can feel his emotion.

"What is this?" My voice sounds foreign to my own ears. Like I've been living underground for years and am just seeing natural light for the first time.

"The report from the night Aaron died in the house fire." He points to the line I kept staring at. "The heater was in the living room."

"But I left it in my bedroom."

"Wouldn't be the first time Aaron went into your room uninvited, would it?"

No, it wouldn't.

My stepfather thought our townhouse was his kingdom and mom and me, his subjects.

Whatever he needed or wanted, he'd look for it anywhere. He used to steal lightbulbs from my bedside table lamps rather than buy new ones for the stove.

He would take my pens I used to write in my journal.

He'd even tried to read my journal until I found a loose floorboard and hid it.

So it's not hard to believe he would have walked into my bedroom when I was out and taken the space heater.

"How..." I gesture to the report. "Did you..."

"Liam put me in contact with a detective on the force in New Orleans. It took a little digging, but he got me what I was asking for."

"But what made you decide to ask for it in the first place?"

"Your story didn't sit right with me. Call it a hunch."

The tears start fast, and they're running down my face before I can attempt to blink them away.

"This is everything," I whisper to him. "Thank you."

His shoulders relax, and he wipes a tear off my cheek. "You know I'll do anything for you, Ashley."

I do know that.

I also know I'm falling in love with him.

But neither of us is ready for that kind of confession.

I lean in and kiss him before straddling his naked body.

We disappear together beneath the sheets as I show him exactly how much he means to me.

CHAPTER TWENTY-NINE

"Hi, sugar."

"Hi, Mama. Guess what?"

"What? You sound excited."

"I'm...well, relieved sounds like a massive understatement."

When I tell her what Jared found out from the report, she bursts into tears. "I can't...it's too much to take in."

We cry together for a minute before she says, "I'm sorry it took so long for the truth to come out. I should have thought to check into it more carefully."

"You were in so much pain, and I was certain it was my fault," I say.

"It's weighed heavy on you all these years," she says. "Nothing I said could put a dent in your guilt. Sugar, tell me, how do you feel now?"

"Like a thousand-pound weight has been lifted off me."

"I'm so glad. How sweet of Jared to pursue that for you."

"Yes."

"Why didn't he try to uncover it before now?"

"He never knew."

She sighs. "Oh, darn it. And I told you not to tell anyone."

I stay silent.

"Ashley, I was worried. With all the guilt you felt, I didn't want you to go around sharing your beliefs about the heater with people. Because all it would take is one nasty comment to send you spiraling even more."

"It made sense at the time," I say. "I do wish I had trusted Jared though."

"Yes, that boy has always had your best interests at heart." I can hear the smile in her voice. "And what's going on with him in Montana? Is being away from home good for you two?"

"Now you're pushing for intel."

"Of course I am. I'm your mama. We always think of our children as our babies. I just want the best for you."

'I know you do. I'm like any person who's been through a rough childhood—I've got some battle scars. It's going to take a strong man to handle me for the long haul."

"You deserve a strong man. You're a strong woman."

"Thank you, Mama. I love you."

"Love you too, sugar. Talk to you soon."

CHAPTER THIRTY

Jared

"I want to take you out."

"Why?" Ashley pouts. "Let's stay in with Louie."

"Because..." I play with her wavy lock of auburn hair as she lies on the couch with her head on my lap and Louie on hers. "I want to go on a date."

"But I like hanging out at our cabin together."

Our cabin.

There she goes again with the possessive.

Possessive is dangerous. And intoxicating. And I want that— to live with Ashley forever somewhere. Anywhere.

But the ranch will do just fine.

We can ride horses and go on hikes and...Christ, I need to stop.

It's only been a week since I showed Ashley the report about her stepfather, but time has flown. We've grown closer, like any barrier we'd been putting up between each other is now gone. It's felt...

Awesome.

Exciting.

And...

Scary as hell.

But the level of desire I have to be with her overwhelms my fear.

We've had sex every night. And every morning. And everywhere.

In the shower.

On the couch.

Against the wall.

In my truck.

And my favorite place...in our bed.

Each time is better than the last. I feel like I'm learning a new part of Ashley's body, and what she likes and what she doesn't, every day.

But as incredible as the sex has been, our outdoor time has suffered. I was supposed to show her around Montana. And I want to remedy that this morning.

"I have an idea." I take her by the shoulders and gently urge her off my lap and into a sitting position. Louie meows and jumps off, heading for her bowl of food in the kitchen. "Today's a rare morning off for me, and better yet, it's the weekend, so you aren't working either. My game's not until tonight. Let's go for a hike on the ranch and then go get steaks in town."

"Won't you get asked for, like, a million autographs and pictures?" She giggles. "I could do a live video of us out on the town for Wild West Ash."

"You'll do nothing of the sort."

She climbs back onto my lap, this time straddling me. "You don't want to be part of my social feed?" she says teasingly.

"I hate social media. You know that."

"But you always say you'll do anything for me."

I grin. "You're a troublemaker today. What's gotten into you?"

She shrugs. "I'm feeling more relaxed. The last few days, I've woken up and not thought I was still in New Orleans."

I kiss her. "How does it feel?"

"Weird. But good. Like I can still be at home even when I'm not at home. You know what I mean?"

Yes, I know exactly what she means. For me, I've got two touchstones—my twin brother and Ashley Hill.

"I love having you here, Ash," I say.

She kisses me back. "Okay, you win. Let's leave our private space and go public."

"You realize we probably won't see a soul on our hike, right?" I tell her. "We're more likely to run into a bear than a human being."

"Don't remind me." She reaches for her purse and pulls out the bear spray. "Mia gave me this. She said to take it with me when I'm in the wilderness."

"It's a real thing," I say. "Running into a bear."

An hour later, we actually do see a black bear ahead of us on the trail. Ashley whips out her bear spray and whispers, "Should I use this?"

"No," I whisper back. "Let's just turn around and go a different route."

We do, and the rest of our hike remains bear-free.

We see a bunch of deer, an elk, and a pair of hawks, and Ashley documents all of it. She's like a little kid at a natural zoo for the first time with her wide eyes and big smile. She jumps around with enthusiasm as she snaps photos with her camera phone, and I tease her that all of her pictures are going to be blurry.

"Just one more," she pleads with me as I stand in front of a massive pine tree. "You look so small. I've never seen you look small before."

"Darling, this is not good for my ego."

She sticks out her tongue. "Oh, please. You could stand to have your ego taken down a peg. You've got a very healthy dose of confidence, Storm."

"Pretty sure that's partly why you love me."

The words slip out.

Why you love me.

Shit.

Ashley freezes, but her hand holding the phone starts shaking.

She covers it up by snapping the photo and shoving the phone into her coat pocket, but the rest of our hike is awkward.

Say something, you asshole.

I can't.

I don't know why.

Something just feels off.

Maybe it's the timing. My brothers arrive in town later today for tonight's game, which means Ashley's girlfriends are coming too. Getting the whole gang back together when she and I are just figuring out where we stand...it's not ideal.

When we get back to my truck, we drive into town, but instead of eating out, we both say at the same time,

"Let's get takeout."

We both laugh.

"You wanted to eat out, I know," Ashley says. "And I would like to do a traditional date. Soon. But not today."

"We'll be out plenty this weekend," I agree. "The usual?"

She smiles. "Yes."

CHAPTER THIRTY-ONE

Ashley

Two hours later, the Mexican food containers are empty on the coffee table, and Jared and I lie naked on the couch underneath the pretty Western-style blanket.

"Come on. It'll be fun." Jared traces his name over my back and kisses my bare shoulder. "You said you couldn't wait to see Win and Peyton."

"That was before."

"Before what?"

He chuckles when I say, "Before Jared."

He runs his tongue across my collarbone, making me shiver. "You were incredible before me, and you're incredible now."

"You're sweet. But I'm not worried about any of that. I just feel awkward with all these people who knew us before we started having sex, and what are we going to tell them?"

"The truth?" he suggests.

"That's a novel concept," I joke.

"What feels weird about it?"

"So we're going to tell them that, yes, we're screwing, but it's temporary, so don't make a big deal when we make out in front of y'all because it won't last?"

A shadow crosses Jared's face.

And then it's gone.

But I recognize the shadow because I've been feeling it too.

Fear.

And the reason I don't call him out on it and try to talk like an actual adult?

I don't know what to say or how to say it.

I'm a successful businesswoman with a lot of life experience, who's lived on my own for years. I've fought my way into a career that I love. But I do not have experience being in a *for-real*, actual relationship where I care *a lot* about the other person.

I care so much for Jared. When he hurts, I hurt. When he's happy, I'm happy.

And when I imagine him hurting me, even if it's unintentional...

I close off.

I can't imagine it, in some ways.

But I know his fears.

I know his walls.

Because they're my fears too.

They're my walls too.

We're so similar, he and I.

I didn't have a plethora of men texting me on the daily, but I'm not famous. And I'm not an athlete.

In my own world, though, I can relate. I had no problems getting dates. Or hookups.

But to purposefully and intentionally go into a relationship with the plan for it to last?

That scares the living fuck out of me.

And that phone call I got yesterday that I haven't told anyone about? That complicates things.

I need to talk to my home girls.

———

"So you and Jared are freaking sleeping together—like sleeping as in *sex* sleeping?" Peyton says in a whisper as she, Winter, and I sit with our heads bent together in Declan's box. The game is at intermission with the score tied one to one.

Storm to Storm as Winter joked since Hunter has a goal for New Orleans and Jared got one for the Wild Kings.

"Yes, Jared and I are...we're intimate."

I smile, and they all envelop me in a hug as they squeal their enthusiasm.

I glance around. Emerson is sitting in the stands tonight with Haley, and Mia isn't here, so it's just Declan and a bunch of other team-related people I don't know. But Jared is their employee, and I don't want them hearing about his personal life from me.

"But..." I stand up and beckon them to follow me to the other side of the box where no one is.

When we reach the empty area on the other side of the bar, I tell them more.

"J and I aren't official."

"So what?" Winter says. "Hunt and I weren't at first either. That will all work itself out. He just has to get comfortable being in a relationship."

"He's not the only one." Peyton's eyes are on me. "When have you ever dated someone seriously?"

"Um, never?" I shrug. "You know me, girls. I don't get into something I can't get out of without a key."

Winter's blue eyes fill with compassion. "Your childhood didn't exactly teach you to trust men."

"Right. Although Jared helped with some old pain. A secret I never shared with y'all."

With the background noise of people cheering, the PA announcer calling out ads, and how much time is left for intermission, I fill in my oldest friends on the space heater and what I believed my role was in Aaron's death. And then I tell them how Jared uncovered the truth.

"I'm so sorry you've suffered all this time and we couldn't help you." Winter hugs me tightly.

"You know what it's like to hold onto shame and a secret," I say to her, and she nods.

Winter's been through her own private hell with an asshole from her Broadway days. She came through it, but she didn't tell any of us for a long time either.

"The Storm brothers are good," Peyton says admiringly. "The fact that Jared would do that for you says so much, Ash."

"He's always been there for me. I'm blessed to have him in my life. But..."

"Oh, no." Peyton wags her finger at me. "Don't *but* this. This story deserves a happy ending with no *buts*."

"It may not be so simple as all that," I say.

"Why not?" Winter says. "You like him, he likes you..."

"I got a call yesterday," I cut her off.

My tone sounds more ominous than I meant for it to, and my friends crowd in closer to me.

"What kind of a call?" Peyton asks me. "From some guy you used to fool around with?"

I wave my hand dismissively. "No, nothing like that. No one could ever hold a candle to Jared anyway. He doesn't have any competition."

"So what was it?" Winter says.

I break the rest of my news. "A head hunter."

Winter raises her eyebrows.

"In the New Orleans area," I add. "She still has my resume on file from when I found out I might lose my job, and then, of course, this position was offered to me, and I took it."

"Head hunters don't usually call just to chat," Peyton says slowly.

"Well, sometimes they will call to feel you out and see if you're still looking. But in this case, she actually has something solid for me. I would be the social director for Mardi Parties."

"Holy shit." Peyton gasps. "That company is iconic in the Big Easy."

"I'd have to nail the interview of course, but she said they're intrigued by my experience and my current social feed. I have a phone interview with them in a couple of days."

"That's huge, Ash," Winter says.

It *is* huge. It would be a big career leap for me.

"Mia's company is well-established and has been very successful," I say, "But this is New Orleans, and the reach is so much bigger."

"This is tough, sugar." Peyton hugs me. "I'm confident you'll do what's right for you, whatever that is."

"Whatever makes you happiest is my best and only advice," Winter says.

She would know. Winter chose to leave Broadway in New York City because she learned she was happiest living at home in New Orleans and performing there instead.

"Life isn't always a straight line," she adds.

Certainly not. And my life's line has been taking me on all sorts of twists and turns. But I had started to feel like it was leading me to Montana. And to Jared.

Just when I was starting to think he and I might have a chance...

I get a shot at a massive leap in my career. Over two thousand miles away. But back home in a place I know with people I adore.

But the man I love is here.

The third period begins, and the three of us file back to our seats to cheer on the Storm brothers.

None of us cheer against either team. Because that would feel wrong. Winter celebrates when Jared and Max do well, and I clap just as hard for Liam and Hunter. Inwardly, of course, Winter's rooting for Hunter to succeed just like I am for Jared.

In the end, the game goes to overtime still tied one to one.

Winter laughs. "Think one of the Storms will win the game with a goal?"

I do. And I hope it's my Storm.

I smile to myself. That has a nice ring to it, calling Jared mine.

I don't want to lose him.

But I don't know if he's actually mine to lose.

Jared

As overtime begins, I face off against my baby brother. I don't think any of the four of us spend enough time recognizing the miracle that is this moment—every year, we get to play on the same ice on the biggest stage for hockey.

"Good luck, Hunt," I say right before the referee drops the puck.

And then, I forget about Hunter and Liam being on the other side. All I care about is the Wild Kings getting the win.

We've been close all game, but now it's overtime, and it's sudden death—first goal wins.

But I've been clutch so far this season, and I don't expect tonight to be any different.

I flick the puck over to Arch, who gets in trouble when Liam checks him hard to the ice. But Tex recovers the puck and sends it over to Max, who immediately launches it across the blue line in my direction.

I cradle it in my stick and skate around the oncoming defender. Liam is barreling toward me, and he's all that stands between me and the goalie.

I know my big brother's tendencies. He's uber-talented and super physical. So, I use his physicality against him. I bait him— I hesitate just long enough to get him to lunge, and then I shift left. My quickness comes in handy as Liam flies past me, just grazing my shoulder. His weight throws me off-balance, but I stay upright and fire the puck toward the goal.

The goalie bites too soon and jumps out left as the puck flies right and into the net.

I raise both hands in victory as my teammates descend upon me. We fall to the ice and pound each other's backs in celebration.

When I finally separate from the group and skate toward the bench, I look up toward Declan's box.

Ashley's clapping and shouting. I raise my stick to her, and she pumps her fist back at me.

I can't wipe the smile off my face.

See you tonight, darling.

CHAPTER THIRTY-TWO

Liam, Max, Hunt, and I have a couple of drinks at a nearby microbrewery to celebrate Hunter's upcoming wedding. Hunt's best friend, Murph, joins us. Murph sometimes jokes that he's like a fifth Storm with all the time he spent at our house growing up.

We catch each other up on what's been going on, and of course, that means Liam and Hunter press for information about Ashley.

"You all know her," I say. "What do you want to hear?"

"We want to hear your side of things," Liam says. "How is the living together thing going?"

"Great," I say. "Louie lives with us too."

Murph laughs. "You're in deep if you're including the cat as part of your family already."

"Hunt and Winter took care of a cat together too," Max says to him.

"Yeah, and look how that turned out." Murph points at Hunter. "He's marrying her."

Hunter chuckles. "I think what Murph is trying to say is that this thing with Ashley sounds more serious than what you're used to, J."

"So what if it is?" I say defensively.

"Then I approve," Hunter says. "You know we all love Ashley."

"And you seem happy." Liam's green eyes assess me. "Are you?"

Yes. Happier than I've ever been.

"I'm...good."

My brothers all grin.

"That's Jared code for yes," Liam says.

"What about you?" I ask Liam. "Have you gotten back out there yet?"

Liam scowls. "Lulu is the only girl in my life. I'm not dating until she turns eighteen."

Hunt, Max, Murph, and I exchange glances.

Liam's marriage to Lulu's mom, Cathy, ended badly, and he's never talked about it. He refuses to talk about it.

"I don't think that's healthy," Max says. "You need adult companionship too, Liam."

"I've got my teammates and you three. I talk to adults all the damn time. Besides, Lulu's more interesting than any other female I've spent time with."

"How are things going with Cathy when you're on the road?" I ask him. "She keeps in contact with you about Lulu?"

"The bare minimum," Liam says.

His jaw ticks, and we all know him well enough to recognize the subject needs to change.

"Well, I appreciate y'all throwing me a bachelor party," Hunter says. "Why don't we go hang with Winter and the girls now? Win just texted that they're bored."

I stand up immediately. "Let's go."

Ashley

"Where are they?" I ask Winter as we sit at the large ushaped booth at Lucky Cowboy. We asked for this booth in anticipation of the Storm brothers' arrival because it's hidden from view by the bar, so the other patrons can't stop by for autographs.

"Hunt texted they're on their way," she says.

Haley and Emerson joined us after the game, and we threw Winter an impromptu bachelorette party. She swore up and down she didn't want anything big, but we still wanted to do something to commemorate the occasion. So I ordered cupcakes from the local bakery in town, and Haley picked them up while we were all at the game and brought them to Lucky Cowboy.

We filled up on burgers and fries and then had the cupcakes for dessert.

"I'm sure the boys have been drinking the night away," Winter says. "I'm so happy we had dinner and dessert. Thank you for the perfect party, besties." She puts her arms around me and Peyton and then blows a kiss to Haley and Emerson. "I'm thrilled you both joined us."

"We've had a great time. You were lovely to invite us." Haley blows Winter a kiss back and then exits the booth. "I'm headed to the ladies' room. Be right back."

A few minutes later, a muscled arm wraps around my shoulders. "Hey."

I break out into shivers as Jared takes the seat next to me at the booth.

Hunter kisses Winter and joins her on the opposite side. Hunt's friend Murph joins them, and Emerson shifts over so Max can squeeze in next to her.

"Great game, boys." Peyton looks around. "Where's the eldest Storm?"

"He's outside on the phone," Jared says. "He'll be along in a minute."

Jared shifts his focus to me. "How was your night?"

"It was great. Congrats on your win." I snuggle in close to him.

He keeps his arm around me even as he reaches for a mug with his other hand. He pours himself a beer from the pitcher on our table and takes a sip.

Then, he stops and looks up at the sea of eyes watching the two of us. Everyone at the table is smiling like proud parents.

"What the hell..." Jared says.

"I warned you they'd be like this," I whisper to him.

"We can hear you," Winter whispers back to me.

Emerson laughs. "Leave them alone," she says. "Let's not make this awkward."

"Little late for that," Jared jokes.

"I don't mind making it awkward," Murph says. "It's too big o' news to pretend it's not happening."

"It is big news."

We all turn and look up at Liam standing at the head of the table like he's the father.

Which, in a sense, he is. He's the only parent among us, and he took it upon himself to make sure his three younger brothers could go to college.

He's green-eyed like Hunter and dark-haired. His expression flips between serious and irritated a lot of the time, but he's got a soft side and a great laugh.

He smiles so genuinely at me that I flush. "You know I approve of this match, right? You've always been the only woman who could handle my brother."

"Hey." Jared glares at him. "You think I'm hard to handle?"

"Obviously," Liam says, unfazed. "We all are. But you're like a stallion that needed taming."

"I don't want to tame Jared," I say. "I like his wild side. And he likes mine."

Liam gives me a head nod. "That's a better way to put it. That's why you two are in a relationship and I'm single."

He says it as a joke, but his smile doesn't reach his eyes.

He slides into the booth next to Jared at the same moment that Haley slides in beside me at the other side of the table.

They both flinch as they look across the table.

Recognition flashes on Liam's face.

"I remember you," he says. "The woman who makes assumptions."

Ouch.

"Hey," Emerson says to Liam. "I know you two didn't hit it off when you met last year, but Haley's a great person."

"It's okay," Haley says to Emerson before she turns to Liam and says in an apologetic tone, "I realize I was rude before, but it wasn't personal."

Liam's hard expression softens just a touch. 'No worries," he says gruffly. "I'm sure I could have handled it better."

Jared jumps in and asks Liam how Lulu is.

"She's awesome," he says with a proud smile. "She's curious and has non-stop energy."

"How old is she?" Haley asks him.

"Two and a half," he says.

"That's a lovely age," she says enthusiastically.

I look at her in surprise. "Do you have experience with kids?"

She nods. "I was a nanny for years."

"Really?" Liam looks at Haley like he's seeing her for the first time. "Did you enjoy it?"

"I loved it. I only worked for one family, and then the kids got too old to need me, and I ended up in the corporate world. Started out as a way to make money, and I found my way to a great company."

Liam's focus is now entirely on Haley. "What company do you work for?"

She blinks behind her cat-framed glasses like she's surprised at his attention. "Same as Ash. Mia Wild's company. I love her foundation because it focuses on rescued horses."

"You like saving animals?"

"Beats trying to save people."

Her blue eyes widen like she definitely didn't mean to reveal that.

Liam puts down the mug of beer he had in his hand. "Why's that?"

I glance at the other guys. All of them are watching Liam and Haley interact like it's a reality TV show and they can't wait to find out the ending.

Haley shifts in her seat like she's suddenly uncomfortable. "Adult people can't be trusted. Animals can."

"Adult people?" Liam's lips twitch like he's fighting a smile.

"Right." She rotates her beer mug around in the condensation it's left on the table. "Children are still innocent."

"Haley definitely backs up her talk," I say, knowing she'll want to kill me, but I can't help being proud of her. "She's so good with the rescued horses on Wild Ranch. And she donates as much of her paycheck as she can afford to protecting wildlife and the environment."

Liam opens his mouth to say something, but Haley spills her beer all over herself. I'm sure it was an accident because her hands are shaking.

"Shoot." She stands up. "What a mess. I'm just going to go home and shower."

"But..." Emerson reaches out to grab Haley. "Max and I will share an Uber with you."

"Oh, don't end your evening on account of my clumsiness." Haley's now ten feet away from the table. "Nice to see everyone. Good night!"

And she's gone. Like a firefly disappearing into the night sky when its light flashes out, Haley Laine knows how to make herself scarce when she wants to.

And whatever sparks were happening between her and Liam Storm, she didn't stick around to see if the fire could sustain itself.

———

The rest of us hang out for a while longer. I admit to being nervous ahead of the night, but being with Jared in front of everyone turns out to be easy. Kind of like how each step he and I have taken seemed like it would be difficult and actually wasn't.

But this interview I have coming up could alter everything once again. I need to tell him about the head hunter's phone call, and I'd love his feedback, but I don't want to ruin his night with his brothers.

I'll tell him after the others fly home.

When we get home that night, Jared is kissing me before we've even unlocked the front door. As soon as the door closes behind us, he crowds me up against it and kisses me senseless.

Our clothes come off in a line across the living room floor, and we end up with me on my hands and knees on the bed and Jared driving into me from behind until I'm moaning out his name while I come and he follows right behind.

We collapse onto the bed, and Jared tucks us both underneath the covers. I lay my head on his bare chest and enjoy the sound of his heartbeat.

Until...

Meow!

"Oh my goodness! We forgot to say hi to Louie!" I bounce up and scoop her into my arms and deposit her on the bed. "I'll go bring in her food bowl. She must be hungry."

When I return with the bowl, Louie happily jumps down and settles in to eat.

Jared chuckles. "Louise, you are one spoiled cat."

"She's not spoiled. She's a queen." I climb back into bed, and my head returns to his chest.

"You're the queen." He plays with my hair, and I nearly purr. "She's a princess. And she's a spoiled one."

"Well, I don't mind. She deserves to be spoiled." I trace my name on his chest with my finger. "Did you have a good time with your brothers?"

"I did. And I had fun with you too," he says. "All of us together like that."

"I was thinking the same thing. It felt like a big step, and yet..."

"And yet not," he finishes for me.

"Exactly."

"You looked like you had something to tell me."

"How..." If I sound shocked, it's because I am. I didn't think I'd given any indication that I had news.

"I know you," he says simply.

"Well, I do have something to share. But I decided to wait until after your brothers leave. I feel more comfortable that way."

"Okay."

He drifts off to sleep then, but I stay awake late into the night.

I'm finally in a healthy, happy relationship, and God decided that now is a good time to offer me a leg up in my career? How is this good timing?

CHAPTER THIRTY-THREE

Winter, Peyton, and I have so much fun shopping for cowboy trinkets for them to bring back home. Emerson joins us for coffee, and then we meet up with the boys at the barn so we can all go on a trail ride together before the New Orleans group leaves for Louisiana tonight.

Jared and Liam are up front with Max and Emerson riding side by side, followed by Hunter. Peyton, Winter, and I lag behind so we can chat.

"So what did Jared say about the job interview?" Winter says to me in a low tone.

"I haven't told him yet." I look over at her. "I thought I'd wait for y'all to leave so, if it doesn't go well, I won't ruin his weekend with his brothers."

"Things will be fine," Peyton says confidently. "You two look solid together. I never thought I'd see Jared in a relationship. It suits him. Because he's with you, Ash."

"We'll see," I murmur. "Jared and I aren't exactly stable rela-tionshippers."

Winter and Peyton laugh, and I do too.

But I'm actually being serious. If anyone could find a way to blow up a good situation, it's us.

Jared

After dinner, Liam and Hunt leave for the airport with Winter and Peyton.

As I say goodbye to Liam, I dare to ask him, "What was that with you and Haley last night?"

"Nothing." He shoots me a hard look, the one he always gives any of us when we tread into his personal life.

Max and Hunter enter our chat, and Hunt laughs. "You think Liam's going to talk about his romantic life?"

"I don't have a romantic life." Liam shoves his hands into his pockets and steps back. "I've got a daughter. She's all I need."

I put up my hands in a surrender gesture. "Just saying that if you ever want Haley's number..."

"J." His green eyes swim with irritation. "Drop it while you still can."

Max puts his hand on Liam's shoulder and steers him toward his truck. "Come on. Let's head to the airport."

Ashley and I wave goodbye as they pull out of Wild Ranch, and then we walk to our cabin.

It's a cool fall day, and the sun is just setting. We sit together on the dock and watch it go all the way down. She rests her head on my shoulder.

"You tired?" I ask her.

"I am. I tossed and turned last night for a while."

"Because of what you need to talk to me about?"

"Yes," she says.

"I want to hear everything, and hopefully I can help. But can I grab a shower first? All I can smell is horse."

She laughs. "That's because you and Hunt insisted on cleaning up the manure pile before we rode."

"And Hunt doesn't know what the hell he's doing. He backed me right into the damn pile."

Still laughing, we stand up and walk arm-in-arm to the cabin.

I give her a kiss and go shower, but when I return to the bedroom, she's already fallen asleep.

I tuck in behind her and follow her into sleep with my arm over her warm body.

She has an in-office meeting with Mia bright and early the next morning, and by the time I wake up, she's already left the cabin.

Meet me for lunch?

I smile at her note with the smiley face at the end. I text her that I'll meet her at her office and treat her to a meal around noon, and then I head in to work.

We have a skate and drills session in preparation for our game tomorrow night.

I skate hard and do the drills even harder.

As I leave the ice, I'm wiping sweat off my brow.

I look up, and Declan is waving to me from outside the locker room doors.

When I reach him, he hands me a key.

"What's this?" I ask, my mind on meeting up with Ashley for lunch.

"Cabin just for you. One opened up early."

I stare at him. "Seriously?"

He holds my gaze. "This is what you wanted, isn't it?"

"I'm not sure he knows what he wants," Max says as he joins us in the corner of the arena.

"This isn't your business," I tell my twin.

He shrugs. "Someone has to tell you what to do. Our parents aren't here."

"You're really going for the bare facts today, aren't you?" I say.

Declan glances between us. "I'm going to leave you two alone. It's cabin twelve!" he adds as he heads for the doors.

Once we're alone, I try to sidestep Max for the locker room, but he stops me.

"Seriously?" I try to go around him.

But Max is a hockey player—he knows how to block.

"I'm not doing this with you right now," I say.

"Then what's your plan?" Max crosses his arms across his chest. "Just move out?"

"None of your damn business."

"Fair. But I hope you have a plan that includes telling Ashley how you feel."

I know he's right.

And I plan to do just that.

But as they say, the best-laid plans...

CHAPTER THIRTY-FOUR

Ashley steps out of the elevator in her work building, and I kiss her hello before we walk through the lobby and over to my truck parked on the curb.

"How was practice?" she asks once we're settled in my truck.

The engine is running, but I don't put the truck in drive.

Ashley's question was clearly innocent, but I'm edgy.

And I can't lie to her. So I say, "Max pissed me off."

"You guys got into it on the ice?"

"Off the ice."

"How come?"

Ashley grew up with us. Me mentioning that Max and I had a fight doesn't faze her.

"Declan told me something that set me off," I say as her phone rings.

She glances at the screen, and her cheeks flush.

She silences the phone and returns her focus to me.

"You were saying?"

"Who was that?" I realize immediately how that sounds. "Of course, it's none of my business. You just...you look upset, Ash."

"I'm not," she says too quickly.

Her phone rings again.

Again, she glances at the screen and silences it.

Her hand shakes as she does so.

Now I'm certain I'm not imagining things.

"Look, Ash. Whoever's calling you is clearly stressing you out. Want to tell me what's going on? Is it your mom?"

"It's not my mom."

"Okay."

She takes a deep breath and locks eyes with me. "It's...a head hunter."

Something about the way she says it has me on alert. Like I'm about to lose the footing I've been enjoying so much since she moved to Montana.

"You're working with a head hunter?"

"I contacted one when I thought I might be laid off."

That makes sense. But why...

"She called me out of the blue a few days ago. You know Mardi Parties?"

"Yeah. That huge company from back home."

"Right. They have an opening for a position and want to talk to me. My head hunter scheduled an interview for this evening."

"An interview for a job based in New Orleans?"

"Yes." She waits for my reaction.

But I'm busy assessing her.

Her eyes are bright, but her hands are clenched like she's nervous.

"Do you want this job?" I ask her softly.

"I adore what I'm doing here," she says, and I can tell she means it. "And I just got here, so I don't want to leave. But this is an incredible opportunity for me because the company is inter-nationally-known. To have their name on my resume would be a huge boost if I ever wanted to open up my own marketing agency."

"It would for sure."

Her eyes lock onto mine. I can read hers as if they were my own.

"Are you worried I'll be upset if you leave Montana?"

I can't believe I'm able to keep the near-panic out of my voice, but I pull it off.

"Well, you and I are..." She cuts off.

This moment could go one of two ways. I could beg her to stay here like I desperately want to do. Or I could let her go to decide on the job of her dreams.

I take out the key Declan handed me not an hour prior.

"It seems like the stars have aligned," I force out.

She furrows her brow. "What do you mean?"

"I mean that I'm moving out. Today."

Her face falls. She recovers quickly, though, and I don't allow myself to second-guess my decision.

Ashley's had too many people holding her back her entire life. I won't do it too. I love her too much to cage her like a bird —the exact thing she fears so much.

"A cabin opened up? Mia never said anything," she says.

"Declan just told me after practice. I guess it was a sign, huh?"

My lungs are tight, but I can't stop now. *Press on, press on.*

"A sign that our time together was coming to an end anyway. Works out well for your career dreams."

"Sure." Her eyes lose that light I love so much.

Now she just looks...vacant and far away, almost like she did after Aaron died.

"Ash..." I want to reach for her, but she recoils like she doesn't want me near her.

"We...we should go to the cabin now and skip lunch. I'll help you pack."

My plan feels like it's in free fall now.

But I have to see it through.

For Ashley.

"Okay. Let's go."

———

Packing up my stuff takes less than an hour. Ashley moves at light speed, especially when it comes to Louie's items.

"You can come visit her. And me." I hold Louie up in her cat carrier, and she meows. "I'm only a ten-minute walk." I hold up my phone and show her where on the ranch Cabin twelve is. "It's right near the barn."

"Great. I hope you're happy there."

She turns me toward the door and practically herds me outside.

My heart is breaking, and as I'm walking out the door, I feel like my plan was a terrible mistake. But Ashley's expression is blank when I turn back to kiss her.

"Goodbye, J." She kisses me fast and shuts the door.

And just like that, the best days of my life are over.

CHAPTER THIRTY-FIVE

Ashley

I wait until Jared drives off in his truck with Louie before I sink down to the floor, lean my back against the closed front door, and burst into tears.

What the heck just happened?

One minute, I was telling him about the potential job in New Orleans—and the next, I was helping him pack to move out of our cabin.

Our cabin.

Not anymore. Now it's just me.

I already miss them.

I miss Louie and her insistent meows and the way she would lead us proudly down to bed for the night with her tail in the air.

I miss Jared and his cocky half-grin followed by his sweet compliments and the sexy way he'd saunter into a room.

I miss his kisses and his jokes and the pillow talk.

I miss spooning with him.

And a good cry is all I can imagine doing.

But I'm in the middle of a work day. And Jared drove us here, which means my car is still at the office.

I text Mia I'm taking a long lunch, and then I crawl into bed and give my heart what it's begging for.

I cry.

Ping!

I peek my head out from under the covers.

Sunshine is streaming into the bedroom, the opposite of how I feel.

Ping!

I reach out and feel around for my phone, answering it without checking who it is.

"Hey!" Haley says. "Where are you?"

"At home. I...fell asleep."

"Are you sick?" Her peppy tone turns to concern.

"Not physically."

"Honey, what's wrong? You sound terrible."

I sit up and try to sound perkier when I say, "I'm okay. Jared...moved out."

"What?!"

"It's for the best, really. I'm..." I realize I can't tell her about my potential job interview before I inform Mia, so I shut my mouth.

"Come back to the office, and we'll get drinks after we finish for the day."

"I'm on my way."

"I would hate to lose you." Mia leans back in her office chair. "You're the perfect fit for our company."

"I love it here too," I say. "This company in New Orleans is one I've had my eye on for years, and I never thought I'd have a chance in hell of working for them."

"I understand. You should follow your heart."

Follow your heart.

Those three words haunt me as I leave her office with the promise to keep her up to date on my situation.

Up until a few weeks ago, following my heart would have meant staying in New Orleans and trying to get in with the best company possible in the city.

But moving to Montana—and accidentally living with Jared —has changed things.

It's changed me.

I return to my office and close the door. Time to put on my interview hat and show Mardi Parties that I'm worth hiring.

"Do you think it's possible for dreams to change?" I ask Haley a couple of hours later as we sit at the Lucky Cowboy bar.

She takes a sip of her whiskey sour before answering me.

"I never thought so before, but lately, I've wondered the same thing."

"Really?"

She nods but doesn't volunteer what brought her to this point. And I don't pry.

Haley's a great person and is becoming a good friend, but I still don't feel like I know her very well. She's private, which I respect. The world could use more Haley Laine's in the world— people who don't feel the need to blabber on about themselves all the time.

Ironically, right now, I'm about to blab.

"Do you want to hear my story?" I ask her.

"Always." Her blue eyes brighten with interest, and she shifts her stool closer to mine.

"Before I tell you, I want to preface by saying that I've already told Mia about the new job interview, so don't worry about feeling you have to keep something from your boss."

Now her eyes widen. "You may be leaving the company already?"

"It's a possibility." I reach for my wine. "It's complicated."

"Well, do tell, Ms. Hill."

So I do. I tell Haley about Jared and the head hunter and the new cabin. And the job interview I just finished an hour ago.

When I'm finished, she exhales. "That's a lot of decisions, Ash."

I finish the last swirl of wine in my glass and signal the bartender for another.

"The strange part is that when I consider dropping out of the selection process for Mardi Parties, I feel an enormous sense of relief."

That's the first time I've practiced saying out loud to another person what I've been feeling since I began my phone interview earlier.

"Did you like the people you spoke with?"

"I did, and because it was a video call, I was able to make eye contact with them and get a better sense of what they're like rather than just hearing a voice. So I really got a feel for the company, and they were all professional and friendly."

"That's all good." Haley pushes her sliding glasses up on her nose. "I'm sure talking to people from home was nice."

"It was."

I change the subject then, and we chat about what our next live video will be about.

"We could go to a rodeo," Ashley suggests.

"That could be interesting."

She starts throwing out different ideas, but my mind is elsewhere.

Because she's given me an idea...

CHAPTER THIRTY-SIX

When I get home to the cabin I used to share with Jared and Louie, I sink down onto the couch and pull up my phone contacts.

Then, I close the tab.

Here's where I'd normally call Win or Peyton and ask for advice. New Orleans Ashley may even call my mom to get their opinions on *my life*.

I'd listen to everybody but myself.

But this is Montana Ashley. Not New Orleans Ashley.

And Wild West Ash is braver than Southern Ash.

Southern Ash was hella brave. She survived an abusive household for most of her childhood. She took care of her mother.

But she didn't take care of her own heart.

That's where Wild West Ash needs to step in and be braver.

I open my social feed.

Fifteen minutes before I go live, I debate over what to do. Text could be missed until it's too late. But I can't call Jared because he'll want to talk.

So I do the next best thing.

I find Max's name in my contacts and press the button.

When he answers, I keep it short—

Tell your twin brother to look at my social.

———

Jared

Cabin twelve is lonely as hell.

Louie's been wandering around the living room meowing since we moved in.

"I miss her too," I say into the empty living room.

Meow!

Louie glares at me and then struts out of the room like she knows I'm to blame for the separation.

Which I am.

I thought I was doing it for Ashley.

Now I'm not so sure.

As I walk around and around the room, staring out the windows at the ranch fields and the majestic mountains beyond, my phone vibrates in my pocket.

Liam's name scrolls across my screen, and I swipe.

"Hey."

"What's up with you?" he says right away.

"Not much. I moved out."

"What?"

"A cabin opened up, and Declan gave me the keys after practice."

"Christ, J." I can hear his disapproval roaring down the line.

"Ash got a surprise job interview in New Orleans. It could be her big break."

"You expect me to believe that you moved out of the cabin you two shared because you were being altruistic?"

"I..."

"Please don't fucking tell me you did it for her."

"That was my intention—to not stand in her way of going after her dream."

"Jared." Liam lowers his voice like he's trying not to yell at me. "Are you pacing right now?"

I stop moving. "What the hell does that have to do with anything?"

"It means you're on edge. Why are you on edge, J?"

I clench my jaw.

"How much are you willing to risk for her?" His voice is soft but the message undeniably clear.

"You're saying I'm being a coward. Fuck you."

Those last two words have no bite to them at all.

Because I know he's right.

"Why?" he asks me. "Why are you running?"

I grip the phone so hard it hurts. "I have no clue how to go about this."

"Go about what?"

"Asking someone I love to be with me."

His exhale sounds an awful lot like relief. "You just do it."

"Just like that?"

"Just like that."

"Thanks for the pep talk, big brother. Someday, maybe one of us can help you as much as you've helped us."

"No need. I've got everything under control."

"Everyone needs somebody sometimes," I tell him.

And right now, Ashley needs me.

Just like I need her.

Liam and I say goodbye, and I finally take a seat.

I lean back on the couch and start scrolling through my phone.

Now that I have a plan, I have to go about putting it into action.

But before I can, Max calls me.

"I'm busy right now..." I start to say.

"Go check out Ash's social."

"What..."

He's already hung up.

I do as he says.

———

Ashley

I set up my camera phone and, without taking time to rehearse, I press record.

As I stare into the camera, at first, the nerves hit me, but then I relax.

"Hi, y'all. For those of you who've been tuning in to my live feeds, this one is going to hit different.

You see, tonight I'm not riding a horse or a mechanical bull.

I'm not doing anything unusual.

But for me, I am.

For Wild West Ash, this video right here is the scariest thing I've ever done.

Deep breath.

The truth is that yes, this Southern lady took a risk moving to Montana.

But the biggest risk was the one I took with my heart when I got here and agreed to be roommates with the boy I've loved my whole life.

I've always been terrified of risking it all in love. I could never figure out why I hadn't clicked with anyone I dated.

Now I know it's because I gave my heart away a long time ago to a boy with dark messy hair, soulful brown eyes, and pain so deep you could drown in it. I carry pain too, but together, we made each other whole again.

He's come through for me in my darkest nights and grayest of days, and his light has always burned so bright I never lost hope in humanity.

So this little video is me being brave, braver than I ever dared to be before.

Looks directly into the camera—

Jared Storm, I love you.

I dare you to please move back into our cabin. I miss you.

I click off the recording and spend the next two minutes shaking.

Texts roll in.

Winter sends a happy screams emoji.

Peyton does the same but adds "so proud of you."

Haley texts me a shocked face and "you did it!"

Mia.

Emerson.

Jamie Beth.

Mama's so proud of you, baby.

But no Storms.

Specifically...

No Jared.

Did he not see it?

I trust Max. He would have made sure Jared got the message.

But...crickets.

Knock, knock.

I suck in a breath, and with shaking hands, I go open the door.

Jared stands before me with one hand full of a cat carrier and the other a bouquet of wildflowers.

"I love you too, Ashley Hill. I always have."

CHAPTER THIRTY-SEVEN

My heart melts.

I melt.

I grab the cat carrier and take Jared's hand to pull him over the threshold.

His hand is cold.

"You're freezing!" I look at what he's wearing. "You're in shorts and a t-shirt? It's cold out tonight!"

"I didn't have time to change," he explains.

We both squat to unzip Louie's carrier so she can be free.

I give her a big hug and kiss her furry head. "I've missed you so much!"

"What about me?"

I look across Louie's back at the handsome man smiling at me.

"Did you miss me, Hill?"

I throw my arms around his neck, and he scoops me into his lap right there on the floor.

"Yes, I missed you, despite the way you sprinted out of here."

He holds me close. "I'm so sorry, Ash. I never want to hold you back, and when you told me about your interview, I..." He tips his head back so he can look at me. "I used it as an excuse to run. The one thing I swore I'd never do."

Jared

"You got scared I'd leave you," Ashley says simply.

"I know."

Her white sweater hangs off one shoulder, revealing creamy skin, and her yoga pants are snug and leave little to the imagination. Her hair is piled high on top of her head with only her usual lock of hair hanging loose. I reach up and tuck it behind her ear. We both laugh when it springs back immediately.

"How come?"

"I didn't think that was the reason I moved out, but underneath, it was lurking."

"Your reaction is understandable," she says. "You lost both your parents. And I've been scared too. We've gotten so close so fast. I wasn't prepared."

"I want you to know that I realized my mistake before I ever saw your video."

She cocks her head. "Really?"

"Really." I kiss her long and hard. "But your video was amazing. You were fearless as always."

"I'm so far from fearless," she says. "I just wanted you to know how much you—and us—mean to me."

"You mean the world to me, Ashley. Living with you here has been the best decision I've ever made."

"And J?"

"Yeah?"

"I'm not taking the job. I'm going to ask to be removed from consideration."

I shake my head. "No way. I want you to take the job if it's the right fit for you. We'll work things out. No matter the miles.

I can live in New Orleans in the off-season. And you can come here to visit. We can do this long-distance. I know we can."

"Maybe we could. But the truth is I don't want to."

"You don't want to what?"

"I don't want to live apart from you when we've waited so long to be together. I don't want to leave my job here. I actually love it. And I don't want to leave Montana, as crazy as that sounds, because I just got here and New Orleans is my home-town. But I love it here, and I'm following my heart here...but I feel like everything I'm doing here is what I'm supposed to be doing and where I'm supposed to be."

"I feel like everything I need is right here in this room," I tell her honestly.

I lean in and kiss her again. Our kiss turns hot and urgent, and she moans as I run my hand over her sweater. She's braless, and her taut nipples poke through the fabric. She straddles me and reaches behind us for her purse.

"Condom," she whispers as she hands it to me.

Within seconds, we're naked. Within minutes, I'm calling out her name as I drive inside her.

"More," she cries out as I give her what she asks for.

And then, she's coming. I flip her over, bend her over the couch cushions, and drive into her again.

I kiss her neck as I reach around to touch her between her legs.

"God, J, that feels so...oh, I'm going to come again..." She drops her head onto the cushion and moans loudly.

And this time, when she goes over the edge, I go with her. Hard.

I'm shaking as I rest my cheek on her bare back and try to gather myself.

That was...

"Incredible."

She took the word right out of my mouth.

And I want more of these nights.

Of this endless love.
Forever.
"Ash?"
"Yeah?"
"I love you."
"I love you more."
Not possible.
But I'll take it.

EPILOGUE

Ashley

"Why are the players filing off the ice?" I ask.

I arrived at the hockey arena early, and I'm sitting in Declan's box with Haley, Emerson, Jamie Beth, and Mia, who's seated next to Declan and Luke Wild.

Haley shrugs. "No idea. Maybe they're going to clean the ice one more time before the game starts?"

Emerson shakes her head. "They never do that this close to game time."

When Jared skates out onto the ice without his helmet, I turn to Emerson. "Why is he out there all alone?"

She furrows her brow. "Did he tell you about some pre-game ceremony the team has planned? Max never mentioned anything."

"He didn't." I crane my neck to get a better look. "The official is handing him a microphone."

"Good evening." Jared's deep voice comes through the mic clearly. "Welcome to the home of the Wild Kings."

The crowd goes wild, no pun intended.

"Before the game begins, I'd like to take a moment here." He pauses and looks at our box.

The Jumbotron shifts the camera to our suite.

Actually, the camera zeroes in on me.

I wave to Jared, my cheeks hot from the attention.

"I fell in love with a girl from my hometown."

"Oh God." I put my hands to my cheeks, which are now flaming.

Beside me, Haley squeezes my arm.

"She made sure I never lost faith. She kept me going when I was lost. And she never gave up on me, even when I'd given up on myself." He skates closer to our box. "Ash, will you come down here?"

I take one step toward the stairs and wipe out.

I pop back up. "That must have looked just great on the Jumbotron," I mutter to Emerson and Haley as they guide me toward the aisle.

"Don't worry about anyone else," Emerson advises me. "Just put one foot in front of the other until you reach Jared."

I do as she says.

The crowd noise is roaring in my ears. I have a brief understanding of what Jared goes through every time he steps into a packed arena, and I have even more admiration for him now.

Because the energy coming at me is overwhelming. I can literally feel it bouncing off of me as I make my way to the rink.

Jared meets me before I have to take my first step onto the ice, thank God, because no doubt I would have face-planted again.

"You okay?" He bends his head to lock eyes with me.

"Yes, but what do you have planned?"

"You'll see."

I put my hand in his, and he leads me back to the middle of the rink and picks up his microphone.

And then, he drops to both knees.

I put my hands to my face.

"I love you Ashley Hill."

I've lost the power of speech, so I just stare at him while he opens a little jewelry box and presents me with a gorgeous diamond ring. "I promise to love you and support you forever. I promise to stay by your side and be your best friend and your partner. Will you do me the honor of marrying me?"

I nod. "Yes."

My voice carries into the mic, and the crowd explodes as Jared stands up and kisses me.

He slides the ring onto my finger, and we hold each other in a tight embrace as we're given a standing ovation.

This is the last thing I ever thought I wanted, a public proposal.

Just like the last thing I thought I'd ever do would be a live video professing my love.

But Jared and I are both learning how to be brave.

With our hearts.

And that's the thing about being brave—sometimes you need to leave your comfort zone and level up.

"I love you, too," I tell him.

Forever.

WHAT'S NEXT

Get ready for LIAM, the oldest Storm brother's story, coming soon!

Take a peek at LIAM:

When I meet Liam Storm the hockey star, a woman just asked him to autograph her bra. I'm not interested in dating a player, and Liam is cocky and flirty and everything I've learned to stay far away from. So I do.

Then I find out he's a single dad. My biggest weakness. But just because he adores his daughter, is a great father, and is gorgeous with green eyes and a sinfully handsome face, still doesn't mean I want to date him.

I can't get involved with a single dad.

So why is our attraction so nuclear?

TO LEARN MORE ABOUT *LIAM,* **CLICK HERE!**

HUNTER

Turns out we both need to score...a second chance, roommates-to-lovers hockey romance.

Hunter

I can't be alone. But I can't be in a relationship. And now I can't even score on the ice. I'm in a slump.

I figure an off-limits pet sitter is just what I need. Until I see who the agency sent me.

Winter Allen is standing all grown up at my front door.

She's my hat-trick: the looks, the heart, and the history.

I let her run off to Broadway because she deserved to follow her teenage dreams as much as I did.

We both got everything we wanted. So why does she look so damn lonely?

Winter

I didn't plan to see Hunter Storm again. And I don't plan to tell him why I'm back home in New Orleans.

But after one devilish grin, my body tells me Hunter's the only man who can help me.

Turns out we both need to score again. So who's to say it's a bad idea to mix his fire and my gasoline?

What are we doing? I'm not sure, but it feels too good to stop.

Keep reading below for a free excerpt!

***

Chapter 1

Hunter

I check the defender hard into the boards and win the battle for the puck.

Spinning around, I cradle the prize with my stick as I skate down the open ice toward the goal.

The goalie pushes out from the net to try to narrow down my angles, but I'm going too fast. With a quick flick of my wrist, I launch the puck off the end of my stick.

It zips past the goalie's outstretched glove but sails wide left and misses the net.

"Fuck," I growl as I race behind the goal.

I slam into the first defender before he reaches my errant shot, and Murph dislodges the puck from between him and the boards. Murph looks up and sees that Liam has a clear path to the net, and he sends the puck toward him. Liam fakes like he's going low with his shot, and at the last second, he flips the puck up past the goalie's stick and into the back of the net.

I breathe out in relief as the buzzer sounds.

"One to nothing," Liam says as he pounds me on the back. "We've still got a shot to win the division."

But when we skate over to the bench and file off the ice, Coach Jones isn't smiling.

"Nice going." Coach slaps Murph and Liam on the shoulders before turning to me. "You do what you need to do to get out of this funk, Storm. You hear me? Whatever it takes. You're our first-line left winger. I want to keep it that way."

His warning isn't subtle, and I know he meant it that way.

"Understood," I tell him. "I'm working through it."

"You need my help, just let me know."

"Yes, sir." I continue past him.

"Whatever it takes, Hunt," Liam says to me as he echoes our family motto. My brother's tone is determined like always. "Right?"

"Right."

Once we're off the ice and out of earshot of any media or coaches, Murph mutters to me, "We need you, Hunt. We got lucky tonight."

Dean, our best defenseman, catches up to us as we head for our lockers. "Fuck, yeah, we did." His blond hair is sweaty and sticking to his head as he removes his helmet and throws it into his locker. "We should have beat those guys going away."

I grimace. This slump has stretched for nearly four weeks. All of January, and now that we've hit February and nothing's changed, I'm starting to panic. But I don't say that.

Prior to January, I'd been having the best season of my career. There was talk of league MVP, and I was stoked. Lately, all that talk has cooled, and I just want to get back to what I know I'm capable of.

It was always my dream to play hockey for my home state of Louisiana—not to mention with my brothers. So when the New Orleans Fire got an expansion team three years ago, and my oldest brother, Liam, and I were picked up, it was a dream come true.

Our twin brothers, Jared and Max, were still under contract for the Montana Wild Kings, but New Orleans was able to snag Camden Murphy out of free agency. Murph is my childhood friend and brother in everything but his last name, and the three of us are feeling pretty damn lucky. We've got a great owner who's all in, and I want to pay him back for bringing me here by playing at an MVP level. But I can't do that unless I get myself out of this damn slump.

I open my locker and toss my helmet onto the shelf. I take off my skates and then start to strip off my jersey and shoulder pads.

"I know what the problem is," a familiar deep, gravelly voice says from my left. "You miss living with me, don't you, baby brother?"

I glance up. Wearing nothing but a towel around his waist, Liam leans against the locker next to mine. He's got his usual obnoxious grin on his ruggedly handsome face.

I cross my arms over my chest and set my jaw as I give my brother a hard look.

"Liam, back the fuck off. I don't need to live with you to get out of my slump."

"Kind of do, man." Murph nods seriously, his overgrown dark hair falling into his eyes.

"We've all got superstitions, right?" Dean says, his dark eyes serious. "Most athletes do. Yours is to have a roommate and make sure you stay the hell away from relationships."

Murph adds, "So how do you manage? Same way I do—you fuck on the regular. You're doing that part just fine. But the first one? Clearly, you need a new roommate." He turns to Liam. "You left him high and dry."

Liam shakes his head. "Wasn't meant that way. He swore he had a new housemate lined up. How was I to know he'd lied?"

"I didn't want you changing your plans for me," I say stubbornly. "I did have someone lined up. But he bailed at the last minute."

"Well, I've got a kid at home—and a wife," Liam says. "And you, Dean, and Murph have got what? Another weekend picking up the flavor of the month?"

I look into my older brother's narrowed green eyes. Sometimes, it's like looking in the mirror. But I'd never tell him that.

"You were just like us until Cathy got pregnant and you two decided to make a go of it," I say, giving it right back to him.

Liam's jaw turns to stone, and he runs his hand through the same dark wavy hair we can both thank our late father for.

"Watch it, little brother," he growls.

I tug at my own hair that's plastered to my head from sweat. "I'm happy for you; don't misunderstand me." I raise my hands in a surrender gesture. "I'm just saying—don't judge me because a part of you still wants to be free and easy."

And...I've touched a nerve.

"I love my kid, okay?" Liam's face is suddenly inches from mine. "And I love my wife. Just because the only girl you ever loved left town..."

I push him into the lockers. He may be older than me, but I've got three inches and twenty pounds on him. Being the tallest in the family comes in handy when you're the youngest of four boys.

"Jesus, Hunt," Liam says as I hold him hostage. "I'm sorry, okay? Winter just pushes all your buttons. She always did."

I press Liam harder against the lockers and pin his arm behind his back. "You better quit talking, big brother."

As usual, he doesn't listen. "Why don't you move on and find a nice girl to settle down with?" he says. "Then you'd have a permanent roommate and wouldn't be screwing up our playoff hopes."

At his last words, I still. "You're clearly not listening. I don't do relationships." Relationships are inherently messy, and I need to put all my focus on my career.

"Hey!" Coach Jones steps into our space and separates me from Liam. "Ease up, Storms. There's media around. You two brothers want to go somewhere private so you can beat the shit out of each other like you're kids again? No problem. But not here. Not when you're with the team."

Coach Jones may not have played in the pros, but he was a star college player, and he's still in excellent shape. He has no problem shoving Liam and me apart, nor any hesitation in giving us both a lethal staredown.

I back off, apologize to Coach, and grab my towel. I peel off the rest of my padding and uniform, wrap the towel around my waist, and head for the showers.

Murph and Dean catch up to me.

"Let's get drinks after this," Murph suggests. "Blow off some steam."

"Can't," I say. "I've got to remedy my living situation, remember?"

"You have a plan?" He raises one dark, bushy eyebrow in surprise.

"Sure I do. I have a pet sitter moving in to care for my cat. I'm gone so much I was paying through the nose for last-minute care by strangers I don't trust to do a good job, and I hate leaving her at a kennel. So, this will take care of two of my problems. Plus, I've got a late night planned with Deb."

"So, you'll get yourself a housemate in the form of a pet sitter, which also resolves your cat care problem." Murph holds up a finger. "And you've got plans with your on and off fuck buddy." He holds up a second finger. "Those two things should kill the slump, right?"

"Right." They better, or I could lose my place on the first line. And worse, we could miss the playoffs altogether. I've worked too damn hard for that to happen.

"Who's the pet sitter?" Dean asks.

I shrug. "Someone who knows the French Quarter. She used to live in New Orleans years ago. I asked for an older lady who won't be impressed by my profession, preferably someone who doesn't follow hockey at all. The agent told me she had it handled, and she's making sure the woman signs an NDA."

"Huh. A chick. Well, as long as you don't fuck her, right?" Dean says. "That will just complicate things."

"I'm not interested in screwing around with a live-in. You guys know that."

Murph shoots me a warning look. "And I know you, Hunt. Just remember, a roommate, even if she's hot, is off-limits."

Chapter 2

Winter

From the backseat of the taxi, I stare out the dirty window at the city lights as the driver weaves his way through New Orleans.

He doesn't drive as crazy fast as the cab drivers in Manhattan, but my stomach's queasy anyway. Must be that fast food I picked up when I got off the plane nearly an hour ago.

I shake my head at myself. Who am I kidding?

My stomach's queasy because of where I'm headed.

Home.

The place I swore I'd never return—New Orleans, Louisiana —where all I ever talked about when I lived here was getting out. Even if I'm only here temporarily, it still feels too long.

In just a few minutes, I'll pay the driver and step out into the heart of New Orleans—the French Quarter. I'll inhale the thick, humid air that reminds me so much of my childhood, air that always maintains a hint of the nearby Mississippi River. I can't deny I've missed the south, but the humidity does nothing good for my hair.

My phone rings just as the driver veers right sharply, and I brace myself to avoid slamming my head against the window.

"Hello, bestie," I say as I answer.

"Yay, you answered! That must mean you've landed!" Peyton's cheery voice comes through the receiver clearly.

I swallow hard, wishing I felt a hundredth as happy as she does living here. Peyton Black has the perfect set-up—she and her boyfriend, Scott, travel the country for months at a time in their motorcoach, and they also spend time visiting his family in Europe. With her business and her parents and brother in New

Orleans, Peyton has the wings and the roots, which is all I ever wanted.

"That's right. I've landed," I say, trying to sound positive.

"Oh, sugar, you're miserable already," she says in concern.

The driver winds through the streets of the French Quarter, and I glance around with interest. It may be nighttime, but the Quarter never sleeps, and people are bustling about the curved streets. The pet sitting job that I applied for is right near here, which was one of the things that drew me to the position. I grew up wishing I could walk around the city at leisure, and this will give me the chance.

"How did your last audition go? The one for the lead on the new Broadway show?" Peyton asks me.

"Um..." I pause. "Not great. It was super competitive."

I don't tell her I bombed that audition, much like the one before, and that was the impetus for my manager insisting I take a few months' break and leave town.

"Your voice is shot, Winter," Pat said. "And you're not the same. Get out of the city for the spring and summer, and come back in the fall for audition season."

"But I can't miss any time here," I protested. We had just met for coffee around the corner from Times Square where Pat delivered the bad news about my latest failed audition. "I just got my big break. That's why I'm getting all these calls. You know that."

We both knew that one more blown audition might cement my reputation as a one-hit-wonder. But Pat was kind enough not to say anything. He just patted my shoulder and told me he'd stay in touch. And then he walked away, leaving me standing on the sidewalk with a half-empty cup of coffee and a nearly-finished career.

"I'm sorry, sugar. Let Scott and me take you out tonight," Peyton says, bringing me out of my thoughts. "We'll meet up with the others and go to the Riverway, not fancy like you and your big-star self are used to with all those Manhattan clubs, but it'll still be fun."

"That sounds great," I say. "But..." I hesitate and cut myself off.

But Peyton's not one of my oldest friends for nothing. "Hunter won't be there," she promises. "Well, I can't swear that he won't be out and about, but everyone knows better than to invite him to come with us when you're going to be there."

I exhale as the cab comes to a stop outside a stand-alone residence.

"But you do know you're going to have to see him sometime," she says gently. "I mean, I know you're returning to New York, but you'll be here for a while, and the Storm brothers are kind of a big deal around here. Especially once the ice hockey team came to town, and Liam and Hunt became its two biggest stars."

"It was easier when he played hockey elsewhere," I murmur. "I could come home and know he wouldn't be around. But now that he's here..."

"I get it." Peyton's voice softens. "But he's definitely here now. And he's pretty much impossible to ignore. You'll see the billboards of the team around the city, and his handsome face is plastered on all of them."

"Have you gone out with him at all?" I never ask her about the boy from my past, but I'd rather know in advance than be surprised later.

"A few times," she says. "My brother's seen him a bunch. And not just at his games." She pauses. "Hunter's party side hasn't exactly let up since you left."

"I'm sure it hasn't. I know I'll have to deal with him eventually. I just need a little time to get my feet down first."

I don't want to admit that seeing Hunter Storm again is the hardest part about returning to New Orleans.

I pay the driver and grab my one small suitcase. The rest of my stuff will be delivered to my parents' house tomorrow, so I'm traveling light. At least I don't have to live with my parents. I'll see them plenty, but the idea of moving back into my childhood bedroom is a bit too much.

I look up at the house before me curiously.

It's freshly painted in white with blue trim and is much better taken care of than I'd expected it to be. I had assumed it would have a barely lived-in feel, because the agent I spoke with explained how the owners are rarely home, but that they don't like to move their cat every time they leave on business. She said the owners are a young couple with a baby and that the man's line of work is rather "unconventional," but she didn't elaborate. And I didn't ask. This is New Orleans—unconventional could mean literally anything.

It's a two-story, townhouse-style home with a cute front porch and upper balcony. Being in the city, it's right next to the neighboring homes, but it has a driveway that leads into the back of the lot, and the entire property has a warm, homey feeling. And the location can't be beat. It's on a quiet side street only a block from Jackson Square.

The agent from the pet sitting service told me the owners would be home to meet me and show me around the place, so I climb the front steps. Catching sight of the sign that reads *Come inside porch to find doorbell*, I push through the screen door and step inside the porch, and that's when I come face to furry face with a handsome, orange-striped cat sitting on a porch swing and looking up at me with interest. I go to give it a quick pat.

"You're a sweetheart," I murmur into the kitty's long fur. "I could definitely take care of you."

The enclosed screen makes more sense now—it's a perfect space for a cat to hang out.

Before I can press the doorbell, I hear the door to the house open, and I straighten up. The wooden door opens outward, and it stands between me and the owner of the house, so I take the few steps around.

And...I suck back my gasp at who's standing in the doorway.
Holy. Shit.

For the first time in ten years, I stare up into the deep green eyes of Hunter Storm.

I immediately start shaking. I don't know if he notices. He seems a little preoccupied staring at my breasts.

He's so...masculine. His eyes are greener than I remembered. His dark, wavy hair's a little more tamed except for one lock that still falls over his forehead. His jaw is set and strong.

And Jesus, he's built. I get that he's a professional athlete, but wow...he's grown up nice. He's all man now.

I watch the muscles in Hunter's forearm flex as he braces his arm against the door. The urging to touch him is too strong, too scary. But God, how I want to.

I picked up the phone to call him a thousand times over the last ten years—when I blew my first audition and was sitting on the steps of my dorm room at NYU, crying my eyes out; when I broke up with three guys in a week because none of them made me feel a millionth of what I felt when I was with him; when I found out backstage I had to replace the lead of Seasonal Bliss and was certain I was going to throw up from terror. And of course, the last time I almost called him when my world was falling apart.

I always dialed his number but then hung up before he answered. And now, he's standing right in front of me.

Holy. Shit.

DOWNLOAD THE REST OF THE STORY **HERE**.

MAX

Fate brought them back together. Will his demons tear them apart? A second chance hockey romance.

Max Storm was my first kiss. My first crush.

And my first heartbreak.

Then, he became a hockey star.

Over a decade later...

I go to a hockey game. And Max accidentally hits me with a puck.

He's there when I regain consciousness.

His chocolate eyes lock onto mine, and I'm a goner.

I just hope that when our time together ends, I'll be able to walk away.

Because time spent with Max Storm is always fleeting...

Keep reading below for a free excerpt!

***

Chapter 1

Emerson

I race through the crowded hockey arena with my camera slung over my shoulder as I follow the moving puck with my gaze. The Montana Wild Kings take control of the puck and push across the blue line, and I freeze in the aisle about ten rows from the ice.

"Hey! Take a seat!" someone yells from behind me.

Without taking my eyes off the action on the ice, I crouch down on the aisle steps and watch as Montana's first-line left-winger and the opposing defenseman bang up against the boards. I'm so close I can hear the players cursing each other out as they fight for the puck. And then—

Crash!

The boards shake as a third player barrels into the fray. He pokes at the puck with his stick, effortlessly dislodging it from the Florida defender's skate and taking off down the ice.

"There he is!" the woman says from the seat next to where I'm crouching.

I inhale a sharp breath. Yes, there he is.

Max Storm.

I haven't seen him in over a decade, and my hands are shaking so much I clench them into fists.

He's no longer the boy I crushed on as a teenager. He's a man now. One thing hasn't changed, though—I'm still the girl on the sidelines, cheering him on while he shines so bright the whole arena can't take their eyes off of him.

"The rumor is Storm won't let any woman touch him," my nosy neighbor shout-whispers.

"He must not date then," her friend says.

"I went on a date with him," a third female says confidently.

I dig my nails into my jeans, using every ounce of willpower not to turn and look over at them.

"Did he let you touch him?" the first woman asks.

Long pause.

I'm dying.

"No," she finally says in a sullen tone. "All he wanted to do was take me as his date to a charity event. He wouldn't even let me put out afterward. I mean, who does that? Look at me!"

Okay, now I sneak a peek.

Yeah, she's pretty. Blonde, tanned, despite it being winter in Montana. And she's confident. She knows she's attractive, and she wears that knowledge all over her fake-bronzed face.

She doesn't even spare me a glance, and I turn back to the ice.

Max may not let anyone touch him now, but he wasn't always that way.

He was my first kiss.

And my first heartbreak.

But that was years ago.

Long before he became a hockey star.

We didn't keep in contact. He has no idea I'm in Montana.

And I don't know if he'd even remember me at all.

That's the last thought I have before Max winds up and fires a shot that ricochets off the defenseman's stick. It heads straight for our section.

I feel cold, hard heaviness hit me square on the forehead.

And then, the world goes dark.

———

Max

Fuck.

I've played hockey my whole life.

I've never once hit someone in the stands.

It would have been a goal if the damn defenseman hadn't deflected the puck. Instead, my shot took somebody out. I stare up at the section where the errant puck went. Between the EMTs and the crowd, I can't see what the hell's going on.

As the refs call a timeout, I rush off the ice and over to the bench.

"Storm, don't go up there!" Coach Tucker warns me. "Let the medical staff handle it."

Fuck that. I toss off my helmet and throw on my skate guards.

"I need to make sure they're all right," I say. "I'll come back in five." I turn and head up the stairs.

The person is hunched over in the aisle. Her long blond hair is covering her face, and I can't tell if she's conscious or not.

I step out of the way as our team doctor hurries ahead and bends down in front of her. After a few minutes of checking in with her, he signals to the two EMTs who are standing with a stretcher.

They carefully lift the woman and place her onto it.

I lean over the stretcher and peer into her face.

With all that blond hair, I can't see much of anything, but as I stare at her, a tightness hits my chest at the same time that warmth fills my body. I can't explain it.

I brush a chunk of her hair off her cheek. "Hey," I say softly. "Are you all right?"

Her eyes flutter open, and she stares up at me.

Gray-blue eyes fix on me in a way no one's have since...

My hand freezes on her hair, and I'm brought back to twelve years ago. "Emmy?"

———

Emerson

The rough touch against my cheek stirs me. I blink my eyes open, shutting them again at the bright lights over my head.

Where am I?

The rough, yet somehow gentle, touch shifts to my hair. It feels good, and I turn closer to it. I open my eyes fully this time and stare straight into the intense brown eyes of—

Max Storm.

His eyes widen in shock. "Emmy?"

He's the only person who's ever called me that. My family and friends call me Emerson or Em, and hearing Emmy come out of Max's mouth flusters me.

"Max. Um...hi." I struggle to sit up.

He puts his hands on my shoulders and gently holds me down. "Don't force it."

He's still bossy as ever, and his face is even more handsome than it was when he was seventeen. But Max Storm the man is more than handsome—he's mesmerizing. From his chocolate brown eyes flecked with green to his midnight hair and square jaw, he could have made quite a living as a model.

His mouth starts moving, and I try to concentrate on his words.

"Sorry—what?" I say.

"Are you all right?" he repeats.

I rub my forehead. Shit, that hurts. "What happened?" I ask, but the image of the puck flying at my face flashes through my mind. "Oh. My. God."

Max's cheeks flush pink. "It's my fault. The puck..."

"I saw the play," I say immediately. "Your shot was perfect. That defenseman slipped. If he hadn't, you would have scored for sure."

"Can't believe how well you read that," he says in an admiring tone.

We stare at each other. "I also can't believe you're here, Emerson Rivers," he says so quietly I almost miss it.

Before I can answer him, the EMT tells me they're taking me to the hospital.

"But I need to photograph the game," I protest. "It's my job!"

"You're here for work?" Max asks me. He looks down at my camera the EMT must have placed next to me on the stretcher. "Give that to me, Emmy. I'll make sure you get your photos."

I reach out, cursing myself when my palm touches his muscled forearm.

He doesn't let any woman touch him.

Electricity zips through my hand, and I jerk back. I try to hide my heated face. "How are you going to do that?" I ask him. "Last I checked, you're going to have a stick in your hands for the next couple of hours, not a camera."

"I'll find a way." He gestures to the camera. "Do I have your permission to borrow this?"

I want to say no, but the EMT guys are already lifting the stretcher. Add *mortified for life* to my resume as the crowd around me simultaneously claps and stares at me.

I nod helplessly at Max. "Go ahead. I'll never live this down anyway."

He picks up my camera and turns to leave.

"Wait!" I call out to Max as I'm being carried away. "You don't have any way to reach me."

He glances back over his shoulder. "I'll find you."

I stare at him. "But how..."

He just winks before turning away. He throws up a hand as he heads down the stairs. "Talk to you soon, Emmy."

DOWNLOAD THE REST OF THE STORY **HERE**.

DECLAN

My one night stand is now my husband ... A MARRIAGE OF CONVENIENCE ROMANCE.

Mia

I don't do professional athletes. And I certainly don't do one-night stands.

But after my father tells me to marry before he'll let me take over his PR firm, which has been my one and only dream since I was a kid, I decide I need a night out.

And when a hot hockey player picks me out at the saloon in the heart of Montana, I decide I want to play.

He takes me to his home on a gorgeous ranch. We steam up the sheets all night long.

And in the morning, I leave him a thank you note and slip out while he's sleeping.

I'm sure I'll never see him again.

Until the next day, when my uncle introduces him as my future husband.

Declan

Before I retire from playing professionally, I'm lining up my next shot—an ownership stake in the Montana Wild Kings hockey team. But the team's got a PR problem, and they'll never approve a bachelor.

I'm not in a relationship. I'm not even dating.

And I can't remember the last time I was interested in someone. Until I go to the bar after the game to blow off some steam and figure out my next move.

That's when I meet her. Mia. The first woman I can remember who doesn't know I'm a big time hockey player.

After we spend an incredible night together, she bails.

I figure that's it.

Until my agent calls me into his office. The only other person in the room? Mia.

My future wife.

We vow to keep our arrangement strictly professional so we both get what we want. But the more we face off, the more I want to score...

Keep reading for a free excerpt!

***

Arch, Tex, Jared, Max, and I slip in through the back of Lucky Cowboy and grab a booth. We might be the only guys here not wearing cowboy hats. I may live on my cousins' Wild Ranch, but I'm no cowboy, and I don't like to fake anything. I've got my baseball cap pulled low on my head, hoping to get through the night unrecognized.

After years of playing in the pros, I've gotten comfortable being approached by strangers for selfies and autographs. But tonight, I'm not in the mood to socialize.

My teammates, on the other hand, are happy to cut loose.

Within the hour, Arch is hanging out with a redhead next to our booth, and Tex is chatting up her blond friend. Jared and Max are in a more serious mood, and I'm right there with them.

"You guys doing all right?" I ask them as Arch and Tex do body shots with the two women a few feet away.

Jared rolls his shoulders. "We will be."

Max tips his glass of whiskey back into his mouth until the glass is empty. "Liam says this will bring us closure. Catching the killer."

"You think it will?" I ask him.

He shrugs. "I'm not as optimistic as my big brother."

I'm not sure what to say to that. The Storm brothers' family situation is so heavy.

"I hope the guy goes to prison for life," I say.

"Thanks, Dec." Jared nods at me appreciatively, and then he glances to his left. "Hey, the blond hottie one booth away is staring at you. I bet she'd be fine with a one-night thing."

I shrug. I've got too much to worry about right now to be thinking about a one-night fuck. But that's just an excuse. The truth is, I can't remember the last time a woman caught my attention. I never thought I'd be thirty-eight and single, but here I am. I want a wife and kids. At least, I always did. But somewhere along the way, my little brother figured his shit out before I did. And now I'm about to become an uncle with no future as a father in sight.

"When did you last go home with someone?" Max asks me.

Too long.

I glance toward the bar. My gaze slides past the hordes of women and snags on—

Her.

A woman with hair so dark it would make a midnight sky look pale; toned, bare legs she's got crossed where she sits on her stool; and the most amazing laugh as she throws her head back in amusement at something her friend just said.

Her friend leaves, and I'm still fixated on her. Which is why, when some asshole pushes into her on his way to the bar, I react.

I'm out of my seat and shoving past Max before I know what

I'm doing. I vaguely hear Jared calling to me, but I'm too focused on rescuing the woman at the bar to stop.

I'm about five steps away from clocking the asshole when I realize she doesn't need saving.

He's got her pinned from behind, and I watch in admiration as she slams her high heel onto the top of his foot. He drops one hand off of her, and she elbows him in the solar plexus, forcing him to drop his other hand. She spins around and jabs a finger in his face.

"That's what you get for touching a woman without permission."

I've reached them now. "Is there a problem?"

The woman turns toward me. "No, thank you."

The man takes one look at me and runs off like the coward he is.

Without thinking first, I reach out and brush a stray hair out of the woman's face. As my fingers lightly touch her soft cheek, a powerful jolt of electricity shoots through me.

Fuck.

I shove my hands into my jeans pockets. "That was impressive handiwork," I say. "You certainly took care of him."

"Self-defense class," she says casually. "My father made me take it."

"Smart dad," I say.

She smiles. I back up to give her room to return to her stool, but as she steps toward it, she stumbles.

She throws out a hand and it connects with my chest. I catch her by the waist to make sure she stays on her feet.

"I'm good," she says quickly. "Thank you."

But she doesn't remove her hand, which is warm against my heart.

I swallow. "Can I buy you a drink?"

She nods. "That would be nice. It's been a day."

Five minutes later, we're seated at a table for two around the corner of the bar. We each have a bottle of beer in front of us. I don't think my teammates can see me from here, but I'm not worried about them interfering. We have an unspoken code between us—if one of us is with a woman, the rest of us know to keep our distance.

"So, what do you do?" I ask her. I purposefully don't ask for her name because I'm not sure where this is going, and I don't want to give out my name if she's only with me for that reason.

"I'm my father's right-hand woman for our family PR firm. He's been supposed to retire for ten years."

I chuckle. "Doesn't want to give up the reins, huh?"

"Bingo." She fixes those blue eyes on me. "What about you?"

I exhale and take off my hat, sure she'll recognize me.

But there's no flicker of recognition in her eyes.

And suddenly, I'm nervous.

I'm so used to puck bunnies pawing at me after games that I've forgotten how to act around a woman who wants to know me as a man and not a hockey player.

"I'm a professional athlete."

I wait for the squealing.

It never comes.

She stares at me. "Are you serious?"

"Yep."

"You play a sport for a living?"

I nod.

"Rodeo?"

I chuckle. "Definitely not."

She smiles. "You don't seem like a rodeo guy. That's the only kind of professional sport I have any clue about. I work with ranchers and cowboys."

"Oh, yeah?"

She nods. "Our company specializes in helping ranchers who want to hold onto their land. We provide different ways for them to bring in money to ease their financial stress."

"That's cool. What kinds of ways?"

"You name it, we've probably tried it. Dude ranches, corporate retreats, parties, and events...I'm in charge of outreach and marketing. I lead presentations to sign new accounts."

"You must be good at what you do." This woman has no issue taking charge—and for once, that gets me even more stirred up.

"It comes naturally to me, I guess. Maybe because I grew up on a ranch, so I get the cowboy mentality." She sucks in a breath as her sky-blue eyes find mine. "I've never dated an athlete, though. Or a cowboy. I've only ever dated corporate guys before. Which is funny because my uncle is a sports agent. But I tend to tune out whenever he talks about his work." She throws her head back again and laughs.

And I want her badly.

"So if you only date corporate types," I say slowly, "that means you normally date people like yourself?"

"Yes. Precisely."

I reach out my hand. "I guess we're opposites then."

As my hand covers hers, the current I felt between us when we touched at the bar is about a thousand times stronger. She feels it, too. I can tell because she noticeably shivers. Her eyes darken, and she flips her hand palm up so we can link our fingers together.

"Opposites, huh?" She swallows noticeably. "That could be interesting."

My dick hardens inside my jeans, and I shift in my chair. "You're beautiful," I say to her, surprised at the stark honesty in my voice.

"Thank you."

"What's your name?" I ask her suddenly, unable to stop myself from wanting to learn more about her.

"Mia."

"I'm Declan."

She smiles at me. "Nice to meet you, Declan."

"Same here."

And then she shocks the hell out of me when she says in nearly a whisper...

"Do you want to get out of here?"

I throw some bills down on the table. "Absolutely."

Get the book here!

ALSO BY MELISSA BELLE

Boston Boys

BOSTON BILLIONAIRE

BOSTON LOVE

BOSTON ESCAPE

BOSTON ROOMIE

BOSTON BAD BOY

BOSTON PLAYER

Wild Men

COLTON

DYLAN

AYDEN

JENSON

BRAYDEN

CAMERON

DECLAN

Wild Men Texas

WHISKEY GIRL

WARRIOR GIRL

WILD GIRL

Storm Brothers

HUNTER

MAX

JARED

LIAM

Bonus Wild Men Stories
WILD MAN (Colton and Sky prequel novella)
WILD VALENTINE (Ayden and Bella short story)

Sign up for Melissa's Newsletter to get a free story and to receive alerts and updates on upcoming book releases.

BONUS FREE WILD MEN STORY!

Ayden and Bella have everything they want...except one thing. Pick up **WILD VALENTINE** as a free bonus short story (complete with an HEA) **HERE**!

STAY UP TO DATE WITH MELISSA

Do you want to stay up to date on awesome sales, upcoming hot releases, and giveaways? Sign up for my VIP List and get a free story!

ABOUT THE AUTHOR

A USA Today Bestselling author, Melissa Belle is known for her contemporary romance style that's sweet, sexy, and smart. She writes hot, steamy romance with complex heroes and heroines. She spent years in the field of psychology before writing her first novel riding the train around Europe with her husband. Melissa likes cupcakes, road trips, and songwriting.

To receive an email when Melissa releases a new book, sign up for her VIP List!

www.melissabellebooks.com